A MAGNOLIA WEDDING

The Red Stiletto Book Club Series

ANNE-MARIE MEYER

ONE

Penny

I loved the smell of new books. The feel of the crisp cover against my fingertips and the inky smell that wafted up from it as I turned the book around in my hand would never get old. I'd been in this business for twenty years, and every time a new shipment of books got delivered to my office, I shut the door, opened the box, and breathed it in.

Today was no different. Jackson Richards' brand-new psychological thriller was a month away from release day, and the box of advanced reader copies had just been delivered to me. I took a sort of pride in the fact that Sampson and Scotts Publishing House always made sure to get my stamp of approval on everything.

I guess when you are named *Editor of the Year* for ten years running, people learn to sit up and take notice.

"How do they look?"

I glanced up to see Harper peek her head around my

office door. My quiet moment was interrupted—never to come back—so I waved her inside. "They look beautiful. Tisha really outdid herself with the cover this time." I ran my fingers along the binding, and a surge of pride pulsed through my veins.

Every book was like my child. I worked so closely with the authors that, by the time the book was ready to release, I felt as if a part of myself was on its way out into the world right alongside the author. And then to see that book excel—priceless.

"I'm so glad to hear that."

I glanced up to see Harper still standing next to me. She had a strange smile, and I could cut the tension in the room with a knife. Something was happening; I just wasn't sure what.

I knew hiring a girl as young and spunky as Harper was a mistake. But I was desperate to appear hip in the eyes of the owners—there was talk of replacing me for someone younger—so I'd made a rash decision and hired her.

I just hadn't realized how hard she'd be gunning for my job.

I'd contemplated firing her. After all, keeping her around felt like keeping an assassin in the spare bedroom. But the publishing world was small, and I had already created a reputation as a hard-nosed witch, which I was desperate to fix.

Firing your assistant never went over well.

So I kept her close. After all, you should keep your

friends close and your enemies closer. And I had no friends. I was the typical, career-obsessed woman. I didn't have time for friends or family.

Not wanting to drag this conversation out any longer than needed, I took in a deep breath, grabbed my glasses from my desk, and forced a smile. "What's up? You look like you need to say something."

Her expression remained stoic even though I could tell that she was celebrating inside. Whatever she was about to tell me, she could barely hold it in. "Mr. Sampson wants to speak to you upstairs."

And there it was. The owners wanted to talk to me.

I refused to show fear as I glanced in the direction she'd waved and then nodded. I grabbed a few books and tucked them under my arms as I headed toward my door. "Ah, they probably want to see the new Jackson Richards book." I stepped through my doorway and then called over my shoulder. "It's going to be a hit!"

I clenched my shaking hand as I waited at the elevator. Every part of my body was quaking. It wasn't normal for Burt or Kyle to call me to their offices. They normally left me alone to work with the high-rolling authors and do my thing.

Lately, however, things had changed. From my twitching fingers, I had a feeling that this summons wasn't a change I was going to like. Even if my mind demanded that I stay calm, my intuition was firing on all eight cylinders. Deep down, I knew I wasn't going to like whatever they had to say.

The elevator's ding rattled around in my mind like a ping-pong ball. Harper had returned to her desk and was typing on her keyboard. I never realized how loud or jarring that sound was until it was only a few feet away.

Pushing away my annoyance toward her—and, let's face it, my life in general—I stepped onto the elevator. I kept my focus trained on the button I'd pressed as I waited for the doors to close. As soon as I was alone, I collapsed against the far wall.

I hated feeling out of control, and right now, I had no idea what was going to happen. I wanted to say that I was safe. That there was no way they would replace me with a younger editor who was more "in *tune with the culture.*" *But* I knew better than to assume that I was safe.

No one was safe. Not in a world where image was just as important as having hundreds of successful books under your belt.

If there was a woman who could sell books like I could but was thirty years younger—they'd replace me in a heartbeat.

It was a dog-eat-dog world here, and I was no exception.

The doors opened on the thirtieth floor, and I stepped out into a large foyer with a reception desk between the two offices. Camilla was sitting there with the phone pressed between her ear and shoulder. She saw me, and I swear her expression dropped.

I wished I could say it was out of fear—a response I'd worked hard to cultivate—but I would be naive to think that was the only emotion in her gaze. Mixed with the fear was…pity.

An emotion I detested.

Not wanting to stand there and be pitied by a receptionist, I squared my shoulders and marched up to her—hoping that I didn't look like an idiot in the process. "The guys summoned me," I said, offering her what I hoped was a confident smile.

If there was one thing my mother had taught me, it was fake it until you make it. I just hoped that was all it would take to dig me out of this hole I seemed to have found myself in.

Camilla nodded. "They're in Mr. Sampson's office." She pointed to the left, and I tapped my fingers on her desk as I nodded.

"Perfect."

I didn't hesitate as I made my way over to the closed door. After a few knocks, I heard a muffled, "Come in," so I pushed open the door and entered.

Burt was sitting at his desk, and Kyle was sitting in one of the armchairs across from him. Kyle was laughing as he leaned over to pick up his coffee mug. Both men turned their attention on me as I stepped closer.

"Penny, please come in and sit down." Burt shifted in his chair as he leaned toward his phone. "Coffee?" Before I could decline, he had his finger on the intercom button. "Camilla, grab a coffee with"—he squinted at me—"two sugars for Penny, please."

I wanted to tell him that I only took cream in my

coffee—an order he'd made for me on many occasions—but decided to ignore it. My nerves were already making me jittery, so a little extra sugar wasn't going to matter. Plus, I would hate for my correction of his coffee order to be the reason they let me go. If I was on thin ice, there was no way I was going to test the waters.

Camilla responded, "Right away." And the room fell silent.

I stood a few feet off from the empty armchair, not quite sure what to do. Was this a catch-up chat, or was this an in-depth conversation that was going to require me to sit down?

Both men looked at ease, so I decided to relax. After all, what could they say that would rattle me? I could take punches. I didn't get to where I was today by playing nice.

"Jackson has disappeared."

I almost choked on my tongue. "I'm sorry, what?"

Burt leaned back in his chair, bouncing a few times as he pressed his fingertips together. His elbows sat on his armrests, and he was tapping his forefingers to his chin. "His sister called today. She said he won't be making any public appearances or attending any signings. He's even contemplating pulling the book altogether."

My entire body felt like a lead weight. I glanced at both men to gauge their reaction. "Where did he go?"

Kyle shrugged. "We're not sure. Naomi wouldn't tell us. She just said he's gone, and she doubts that he'll come back."

I blinked as I clutched the copies of Jackson's latest book to my chest like they were my life raft—which felt oddly poetic. They were the only thing keeping me afloat as I watched my career crumble before me, and yet they were also causing me to sink into the bleak abyss that was my life. If Sampson and Scotts was looking for a reason to dump me, losing my star author would be reason number one.

"That's so strange. I spoke to him last week, and he seemed ready for release." I managed to speak with a small level of decorum. I was panicked, but I needed Burt and Kyle not to know that.

Burt's chair squeaked as he rocked back. The motion mixed with the sound was like a siren in my mind. I needed a scotch and some Advil with the way my head was pounding.

"Well, he's gone. With a book releasing in less than a month…" He clicked his tongue as if that was the only response he needed to give me. The silence filled in his meaning.

If I couldn't get Jackson back here and on board with what he needed to do, I was out. Gone. Fired.

My throat felt dry as Camilla snuck in and handed me the mug of coffee. Not caring what the two sugars would do to my hips, I sipped the warm liquid. I needed to calm down. The hurricane of emotions inside of me felt as if it was going to swallow me whole.

With the moisture from the coffee mixed with my inability to fail, I forced all of my strength to the surface and spoke with what dignity I had left. "I'll take care of it."

Burt flicked his gaze over to Kyle before bringing it back to me. He was silent for a moment before he nodded. "That's what I like to hear. Fix this little issue, and we'll reevaluate."

Not wanting to tuck my tail between my legs and run from his office, I squared my shoulders and nodded. "It'll be a blip on the radar." I was just going to sidestep his last comment and pretend that my career wasn't currently on the chopping block.

I stepped forward and dropped the books on Burt's desk. "Thought you guys might like a copy of Jackson's book. He really knocked it out of the park on this one." I tapped the cover. "It'll be a best seller, mark my words."

Burt leaned forward and pulled the books toward him. He picked one up and riffled through the pages before setting it back down. I hated to see how he manhandled the book. The reverence that I felt for the written word was not reflected in his gaze. He saw the book as a money maker; I saw the book as a living, breathing entity. The soul of an author portrayed for the world to read and judge. It was no small feat.

Even though I was frustrated with what Jackson was doing to me, I understood the soul-crushing fear that comes with writing.

Once I reamed him out for leaving me in the lurch like this, I'd allow myself to pity him—but only then.

"I hope so," Burt said. His tone didn't invite more conversation, and I knew that our meeting was over.

It was my job to find Jackson and return him. Burt's meaning wasn't lost on me. I needed to bring him back and cultivate a best seller if I wanted a chance at saving my career.

I wasn't going to fail.

I left the minute I got back to my office. After setting my phone to go straight to voicemail, I let Harper know that she could reach me on my cell and headed down the elevator to the rideshare that was waiting for me.

Back in my apartment, I packed my suitcase as I tried Naomi. She didn't pick up, and after my twentieth call, I gave up. I located Jackson's address in the paperwork I had for him and headed to JFK, where I bought the first ticket I could to North Carolina.

The sun was just starting to set when my taxi pulled into the driveway of a small rambler. I paid and stepped out of the car. There were a few lights on in the house, which helped me feel more confident that this nightmare was almost over.

I'd find Jackson and drag him back to New York kicking and screaming if I had to. There was no way I was going to take no for an answer.

With my suitcase dragging behind me, I made my way to the front door and rang the doorbell.

The wait was excruciating. I hadn't eaten anything since breakfast, and I was exhausted. I wanted to get this

problem solved so I could focus on my rapidly disap-
pearing career.

Even though it felt like I waited a lifetime for the door
to open, realistically it had only been a few seconds. The
door swung open to reveal a slender woman with blonde
hair and glasses perched on her nose. Her eyebrows rose
as her gaze swept over me.

"Does Jackson Richards live here?" I asked.

The woman folded her arms as she studied me. "And
you are?"

Taking that as a yes, I reached into my purse and
pulled out my business card. "I'm his editor, and I'm
looking for him."

The woman took the card. She studied it for a
moment before she slipped it onto the side table next to
her and returned her attention to me. "This is his home,
but he isn't here right now."

My hope that this nightmare was over deflated like a
balloon. "Where is he?"

The woman studied me. Then she sighed. "I'm not
sure. I have a few places he could be, but when he gets
like this, he just…disappears."

I pressed the bridge of my nose between my fingertips. My headache was raging now. The woman seemed
to take in my state as she leaned forward and grabbed the
handle of my suitcase. Before I could stop her, she
pushed open the door and waved me inside.

"Why don't you come in, and we'll figure it out. I

have some spaghetti on the stove, and I made way too much for one person to eat."

The smell of oregano and tomato sauce wafted out and made my mouth water. My stomach growled. As much as I wanted to thank her for her kindness and continue my search, I knew if I didn't eat soon, I'd collapse. It had happened on a few occasions when I'd worked for too long without eating.

If I was going to face Jackson and convince him of anything, I needed a full belly.

"Thanks…"

"Naomi."

"Naomi."

She smiled as she shut the door behind me. Then she waved me toward the kitchen and sat me down at the table as she bustled around, grabbing me a glass of water and setting a plate in front of me. I thanked her as the desire to get up to help her was overshadowed by my utter exhaustion.

Searching high and low for an author would take it out of anyone, but the additional stress of my job being on the line made me feel as if I would crumble.

Thankfully, a full stomach solved a lot. By the time I pushed my empty plate away from me and dabbed my lips, the world felt a little less crappy, and I felt a little more optimistic about my future.

Naomi seemed more relaxed as she brought her feet up onto the chair next to her and studied me. Feeling as if I were under the microscope, I shifted in my seat. I was a control freak, but in this moment, I felt anything but in control.

"Why did he run?" I asked as I fiddled with my fork, which I'd placed on my plate.

Naomi sighed. "That's Jackson. Anytime he gets overwhelmed or stressed, he just shuts down." She massaged her temples. "It makes it hard to be his sister."

"But you think we can find him?" I needed some hope right now.

Naomi dropped her hands and then nodded. "He'll turn up."

Just as she said the words, her phone chimed. She straightened and glanced down. I saw her eyes move as she read the message. I wanted to know if it was about Jackson but didn't want to overstep. So I settled on clutching the napkin in my lap for dear life while I waited.

A moment later, Naomi looked up and gave me a smile. "I found him."

"Where is he?" I winced at how eager I sounded.

Naomi furrowed her brow. "A town called Magnolia."

TWO

Fiona

(Day after Maggie's Engagement Party)

"*J* will have a tall sweetened double-shot on ice with almond milk?" Tessa read off the order from her phone and then glanced up at me. The way her voice rose after she said "milk" made me wonder if she was asking me a question or if that was what she wanted.

I decided to go with it and proceeded to write her order down.

"Does that sound good? I don't know." Tessa blew out her breath as she leaned against the counter on one arm. "My daughter sent this to me. Said it would be healthier than what I normally drink." She tucked some of her wild white hair behind her ear. "But now that I say it out loud, all those words sound foreign to me."

I laughed as I grabbed a nearby cup and shook my

head. "It sounds great. I'll whip it up, and you'll have to tell me what you think."

Tessa's nervous expression faded away as she nodded. "Okay. I like that idea."

I shot her a smile as I started working, reveling in the distraction of making Tessa's drink. My stomach was in knots. Austin, my lawyer and Shari's brother, was coming into Magnolia today to meet with me. After I suggested mediation to Dave and got absolutely nowhere, I began to realize that I was going to need to be bolder and more assertive if I was going to get my ex to do what he was supposed to.

I didn't like being confrontational, and the last thing I needed was more stress in my life, but I'd opened this Pandora's box. I needed to see it through. Even if, at this moment, I felt like a bundle of nerves wrapped in skin. I was anxious, and that did nothing for my mental or physical health.

I was still trying to find a new job that paid more than the coffee shop and allowed me to be flexible with Blake. I was struggling with sleeping at night. I had no appetite, and I was constantly on the verge of tears. In short, I was a mess.

I swallowed back my emotions as I handed Tessa her drink. She took it graciously and after a few sips smiled back at me. "This is delicious," she said and then took another long drink.

I leaned against the counter and smiled. "I'm glad you like it." I needed this morale boost even though it seemed tiny and insignificant. At least it proved that I could do something right. Making coffee seemed to be the only job I was good at. As much as I loved the smell of freshly ground coffee beans, it didn't pay like I needed it to. I studied Tessa. Maybe she knew of someone who was hiring. "Hey, Tessa?"

She turned to face me. Her lips were still locked on the straw, but her eyebrows rose to acknowledge that she'd heard me.

"I'm looking for a job. Have you heard of anyone who's hiring?"

Tessa swallowed and lowered her drink. Her eyebrows furrowed as she squinted her eyes. "I haven't, no." She held up her cup. "But you make such good stuff, why would you need another job?"

I wasn't sure how much Mom wanted people to know about her financial troubles, so I decided to be as discreet as I could. I shrugged and grabbed a washcloth to wipe the counter down. "I just need something that is more permanent." I paused and glanced over at Tessa. "I can't work here forever. Mom can only support me and Blake for so long." I hoped my relaxed smile told her that I wasn't stressed about it and only wanted something different.

She studied me for a moment before she nodded. "If I hear of anything, I'll let you know."

Relief filled my chest. That was all I could ask of her. If I put out enough feelers, something had to come of it all.

The afternoon came and went. There was a constant trickle of people that kept me busy enough to be distracted. Just as I would start to dive deep into my depression over what I was going to do about my situation, a patron would enter, and I would have something else to focus on. It was nice but definitely not sustainable. By the time Maggie walked into the shop, I was exhausted.

Maggie looked just like I felt. Worn out and tired.

"Coffee?" I asked as she stepped up to the counter.

She nodded with a pleading gaze.

I shot her a sympathetic smile as I poured her a cup and pressed on the lid. "On the house."

She thanked me.

"How's it going with your mom here?" I asked, knowing that she and Penny had a strained relationship. I didn't know too much about the situation, but it had to be hard on Maggie.

She blew out her breath. Her response looked as if it was going to be a story. I glanced around to see that the shop was pretty much empty, so I rounded the counter and led her over to an empty table. We both collapsed on the chairs and sat in silence for a few minutes before Maggie spoke.

"It's exhausting. I never realized how hard it is to have a conversation with my mother." She tucked some of her blonde hair back up into her bun.

"It's that bad, huh?"

She nodded. "I mean, I love my mother because the

woman gave birth to me. But she is testing me in ways I have never been tested before." She rubbed her temple with her free hand. "Archer and I want a simple wedding on the beach. We want it to happen soon. All the people we care about are here, so why wait."

I nodded. "Makes sense." Maggie didn't strike me as the fancy, wait-for-years-to-get-married type of girl.

"I know what I want, and I want Archer. I want to marry him." Her cheeks flushed as she leaned in. "We want kids."

My heart surged at her words. Even though raising Blake was stressful, and dealing with Dave was stressful, I would never give up being a mom. I wanted that for Maggie. Plus, after hearing about what had happened to Archer's daughter, I wanted it even more for him.

"I'm not getting any younger. If we are going to do this, why wait?"

"Your mom wants you to wait?"

Maggie shrugged. "I don't know what my mom wants. She's so wrapped up with her issues with Jackson Richards that she's not being direct. But she's sighing at every choice I make." Maggie rested her hand on the table and then drummed her fingers. "I have half a mind to just go to the justice of the peace tomorrow and wed that man. I don't need a fancy dress or a five-tier cake. I had that wedding once. It didn't last. I really don't need it again."

As much as I understood where Maggie was coming from, I knew that if she did something on a whim, she was going to regret it. I reached out and patted her hand. "Go home and take a bath. Get some rest and then decide in the morning."

Maggie sighed as she took another sip of her coffee. "You're right. I shouldn't do anything too rash."

I shook my head. "And if you need help in the morning, I'm more than willing to play some Mom defense so you can get a break."

The tears that I saw forming in Maggie's eyes caused tears to prick in my own. I blinked a few times, forcing them to retreat. This was not the time to start crying. I was fairly certain that if I did, Maggie would follow shortly after. The last thing this coffee shop needed was two sobbing women, front and center.

Needing a break from my emotions, I leaned back in my chair. "Any chance you've heard of a job opening?"

Maggie grabbed a nearby napkin and began to wipe her eyes. Then she blew her nose and focused her attention back on me. "The shop still struggling?" she asked, her voice a whisper.

I glanced around just to make sure no one was listening and then nodded. "Yeah. Mom doesn't say anything, but I know she's stressed. I just want to do something more for her, you know? Plus, there's my new legal fees. I know she's going to want to cover them, but the dollars just don't add up."

Maggie nodded as she grabbed a new tissue and began to fold it in her hand. I could tell that she was thinking, and a moment later, it was as if a lightbulb had gone off. She sat up a bit straighter. She was excited about something.

After digging around in her purse, she emerged with a pen and held it up like a lightsaber. She grabbed a fresh napkin and started writing on it. "My mom is here to convince one of her authors to go back to New York. I heard her say that he was looking for a housekeeper-slash-chef. You should go talk to him." She clicked her pen and then slid the napkin over to me.

My gaze roamed over her handwriting. I recognized the street name, but I wasn't sure where exactly he was staying. But it was a lead and the only one I had.

"Great. Thanks. I've got a meeting with Austin, but I'll head over after. Shari and Danny have Blake for me today. I'll see if she can keep him a bit longer." Then I laughed as I thought about all the tantrums I had to endure the last time I dragged him away from Shari and her kids. "I doubt he'll even miss me."

"Shari does love Blake. She's always talking about him." Maggie sighed. "I'm glad you moved here."

My emotions went haywire again, and I moved to stand. I needed to focus on my upcoming meeting with Austin as well as showing up at Jackson Richards' house, begging him for a job. I wasn't the best housekeeper or chef, but I would try my hardest if that meant I was going to be able to make more money to give to Mom.

It was time I pulled my weight around here.

AUSTIN LEFT an hour after he arrived. He was optimistic that things would go smoothly with the judge and we would have an open-and-shut case. The DNA test we ran proved that Dave was the father—which I knew despite what he said about me—but we needed to get one with his consent.

Thankfully, Austin knew how to take care of that and told me to relax, and it was in his hands. Which I was grateful for. Ever since I went down to Nashville to confront Dave, I'd been a stressed mess.

I went between freaking out about money to crying into a bucket of ice cream every time I thought about my past. I had loved Dave, and deep down, I knew I was always going to love him. Which only made all of this that much worse.

The pain was that much more poignant.

Thankfully, Shari agreed to watch Blake a little longer. She even offered to feed, bathe, and pajama the kid. I thanked her, my tears once again choking my throat. If I didn't get a handle on my emotions, I was going to break down into tears in front of my potential employer.

Mom took over the shop, and I raced upstairs and changed. Not sure what a housekeeper/chef wears, I went with a basic red T-shirt and jeans. I swiped on some mascara and ChapStick, grabbed Mom's car keys, and hurried outside with Mom yelling, "Good luck!" behind me.

I threw a quick wave in her direction, unlocked the

car door, and climbed in.

The drive took about twenty minutes. Apparently, he lived on the other side of the island. I took note of the distance. It wasn't ideal, but if the pay made up for the drive, I'd be set.

The house was set on a peninsula. The road turned into a driveway, and my headlights flashed against the weathered white siding as I pulled up to the house. There were a few lights on which shone against the dark sky.

I'd seen enough murder mysteries to know that I should be suspicious of this place. Who exactly was this man, and how did Maggie know him? I grabbed my mace and held it in my hand. I trusted that Maggie wouldn't send me into a serial killer's house, but that's how they always get you—when you least expect it.

As soon as I stepped out of the car and slammed the door, the sound of the waves crashing onto the shore filled my ears. The air smelled of salt, and I could feel its sticky fingers as it snaked around my skin, which only added to the eeriness of this place.

I could literally hear the low music that always played in the background when the main character approached the murder scene. Then, feeling completely stupid, I straightened and pushed that thought from my mind. What was the matter with me?

I was an adult. Not everything around me was a story. He was probably an old man with absolutely nothing interesting about him.

I rounded the house to find that the front door faced

the ocean. I walked along the porch that spanned the entire house until I was standing in front of the double doors. I could see that there were a few lights on in the kitchen, but other than that, the house was dark.

Just as I raised my hand to knock, the door swung open, and I was confronted by a pale-faced Penny. She looked irritated and stressed as her gaze swept over me.

"What are you doing here?" she asked, her voice taking a bitter tone that surprised me. She always tried to be nice in town.

Not sure what was going on, I parted my lips but wasn't able to utter a word before a tall, dark-haired man appeared in the doorway behind her.

"I told you, Penny, I'm not coming back. I'm not—" His voice cut off when his gaze landed on me. His frown turned deeper as he studied me before turning to Penny. "I don't care about the money. I'm done."

Penny turned to face me. Her lips were parted, and I could tell that she had a lot she wanted to say, but nothing was coming out. The man—who I could only assume was Jackson—kept his gaze trained on her. Feeling awkward standing in the middle of this show-down, I slunk into the corner of the porch, wishing that a hole would open up and swallow me.

It took a moment for Penny to sigh and break her stare. She glanced around as she rubbed her temples. "There has to be something I can do to convince you to change your mind."

"There's not. Now go away."

I wanted to step in and defend Penny. Even though she could be harsh, I could tell that his words were breaking her down. Just as I stepped forward, she sighed once more and nodded.

"I'll be back tomorrow."

"And my answer will be the same."

"Regardless, I'll be here." She turned, her shoulders sagging as she rounded the house, and was gone.

Jackson stood in the doorway for a moment, his gaze trained on the ocean. I could tell there was a storm raging inside of him; I just wasn't sure what any of it meant. Or if it was even my place to ask.

"Who are you, and what do you want?"

It took me a moment to register that he'd spoken to me. His voice was low, and he was still staring out at the water. I stumbled forward.

Slowly, he brought his gaze over to me. His dark blue eyes were like the sea at night. There was a pain in his demeanor that took my breath away. My entire body shivered under his scrutiny.

"I'm, um…" I swallowed, my throat going dry.

He raised an eyebrow, and as he did, his face tipped, and I saw a jagged scar down his left cheek. It startled me. He must have noticed me staring because, a moment later, he dropped his head back down.

"I don't buy cookies," he said as he turned to move back into the house.

That pulled me from my stupor. I blinked as I hurried after him. "I'm not…" I stopped in front of the door before he could close it fully. "I'm not a Girl Scout."

Jackson stopped, his back to me. His shoulders were sagging as if he were carrying the weight of the world. Then a moment later, he lifted his head and said over his shoulder, "Yeah, it was a joke."

"Oh." Then I forced a laugh. He needed to see that I was not as stupid as I sounded. "I'm Fiona."

He turned and held the door mostly closed so that all I could see was the middle of his chest and his face. "Fiona?"

I nodded. This was going *fantastic*. "Yes. I'm here to apply for the job."

He furrowed his brow. "Job?"

I swallowed again, praying that my mouth would moisten. "Maggie said you were looking for a house-keeper-slash-chef."

"Housekeeper-slash-chef?" he repeated.

I wasn't sure how to analyze our conversation. He was either insulting me or repeating what I said because we spoke two different languages. Gathering what dignity I had left, I sucked in my breath and plowed forward.

"I would like to be considered for the job. Although I don't have a ton of experience, I am a hard worker and learn quickly." I reached into my pocket where I'd stashed the piece of paper with my name and phone number.

I shoved it into his hand, not waiting to see if he grabbed it or not. I needed to get out of here, run back to my car, drive away, and never look back. I couldn't imagine ever showing my face around Jackson Richards again.

My feet took off before my brain could catch up. I kept the pace until I slammed the driver's door shut and threw the car into reverse. I didn't realize that my hands had a death grip on the wheel until I was a good five minutes from the house.

I must have looked like a crazed woman when I got back to the coffee shop because Mom wouldn't take her gaze off of me. She followed me as I hung my purse up on the hook in the back. I blew out my breath as I took in her expectant look and attempted a weak smile.

"You look like you've just seen a ghost. Where did you go?"

I shook my head as I grabbed my apron. I was going to help her clean up until Shari arrived, and then I'd focus on Blake. "It doesn't matter 'cause I'm never going back," I said as I pushed back out into the shop.

Before Mom could respond, my phone chimed. She waited for me to pull it from my pocket. I figured it was Shari with an ETA on Blake. What I found made my entire stomach drop.

Unknown Number: This is Jackson. Be here at 8 a.m. sharp.

THREE

Penny
---

 *N*othing was going my way.

    I'm not sure why I thought coming to Magnolia and confronting Jackson would solve anything. But I did it anyway, and I was regretting it. Nothing I'd said to him when I showed up at his house a few hours ago had changed his mind.

He was pulling his book and getting out of the publishing world, period.

I'd tried to convince him, threaten him, and bribe him. Nothing worked. He didn't care if he was going to have to pay back his advance. He didn't care that he was never going to work in the publishing world again. And he didn't care that his leaving would ruin my career. He was done. It became clear that no matter what I said to him, he wasn't going to change his mind.

I blew out my breath as I sat at a table in the corner of the dining room at the inn. The room was sparsely populated, which made me feel better. I liked to wallow in solitude. I didn't want people around me when I was this low.

I had an image to uphold. I could only imagine what the media would say if they found out the great Penny Brown had been brought so low. There were so many gunning for my job that it would be only a matter of time before Burt and Kyle found yet another reason to let me go.

"Bad day?" a deep voice asked me.

I turned to see Brett, the inn's chef, standing behind me. He had a mug in one hand and a plate full of cookies in the other.

"If you only knew," I said as I turned my attention back to the table. I didn't want to talk about my feelings or struggles, and I certainly didn't want to be pitied. I was going to sit here until I came up with something that would get Jackson to come back.

There had to be something.

After Naomi got the text from Jackson's friend—who was the new sheriff of Magnolia—that Jackson was there, I hurried back to New York to let Burt and Kyle know. I finished a few projects and found a dog sitter before I made my way to Magnolia. I just happened to find the entire town at some dance studio, celebrating the engagement of my daughter—that I had no clue was even taking place.

I was at my lowest low with an entire town staring back at me as I'd announced that I was staying in

Magnolia. I didn't really care about the town's reaction; after all, these were people that I wrote out of my life a long time ago. But seeing the strained look in my daughter's eyes hurt.

Why didn't I know that Archer had proposed? Did she call me, and I just missed it? The guilt that overtook me was hard to ignore.

"You seem distracted, so I'm going to just leave these here," Brett said, moving to set the cookies and coffee down in front of me, but waiting for my approval.

I grabbed his hand just as he started to pull it away. "Oatmeal raisin?"

Brett chuckled. "Maggie ordered that I whip up a batch just for you."

My heart softened at those words. Maggie and I may have a strained relationship, but I knew she cared about me. A lot. "Keep them coming, then," I said as I released his hand.

I was midway through my third cookie when a familiar raspy voice said, "Well, aren't you a sight for sore eyes."

I turned to see Debbie Swanson standing next to my table. Her pure white hair was pulled back into a bun, and she had a pair of black readers on her nose. I inhaled at the sight of my mom's best friend, and just as I did, a crumb flew to the back of my throat.

It took a hot minute, but I was finally able to dislodge it. I took a large gulp of hot coffee and offered her a weak, "Hi," in response.

That must have been exactly what Debbie needed for an invitation because, a moment later, she'd slipped onto the seat across from me and picked up a cookie. "I haven't seen little Penny Anne in years," she said as she broke off a piece of cookie and slipped it into her mouth.

My eyes were watering from my cookie crumb ordeal, and I was fairly certain that if I spoke, I would sound like a chain smoker. So I just nodded along as she continued.

"How are you doing? I'm so glad to see you again. I think the last time we spoke was at Dorthy's funeral?"

The mention of my mother made my stomach churn. I offered her a weak smile, praying that she wouldn't push this further. But with Debbie Swanson, discretion wasn't a luxury afforded to me. She was going to talk about what she wanted to talk about. Period.

"I miss that woman. She had some spunk in her. I fear with her gone, I'm turning into a sad sack of rolls and skin." Debbie chuckled at her joke, and I just continued to smile.

After all, what was I supposed to say?

"Are you here for long?"

My throat ached, but it felt better enough to actually respond. "Hopefully just a few days." But with Jackson, I knew realistically it was going to be a few weeks.

We did have three months until the book was scheduled to launch. So there was plenty of time to change his mind. All I needed to do was stay focused and dedicated. If I did those two things I would be on the road back to New York in no time.

"That's too bad. I was hoping your stay would be longer." Debbie's phone chimed, and she flipped it open. "My grandkids keep wanting to buy me a touchscreen phone, and I tell them I like what I have, thank you very much."

I just nodded. She must get asked about her phone on the regular. Her response felt almost like a reflex.

"Ah, it's Vivian. I should take this."

Ready to be alone, I nodded and held out my hand as if I needed to signal that she was free to go. It took a few seconds for her to stand, but when she did, she moved over to wrap her arm around my shoulders and give me a squeeze. After planting a kiss on my cheek, she pulled back.

"I know Dorthy would have wanted to see you come back even for a short period of time. She was always so proud of you making a name for yourself in that big city. We missed seeing all your articles in the paper. I know Dorthy kept a pile in her living room up until the day she passed." Her eyes filled with tears, which made my own do the same.

Not wanting to break down here in the inn's dining room, I just nodded and took a sip of my coffee. I needed something to distract me. There was no way I wanted to start crying in front of Debbie. She was sweet, but she had loose lips. I had a reputation to uphold.

Plus, my old job and love of my life—the town's newspaper—wasn't a memory I was quite ready to revisit. So much had happened to me when I wrote for the paper. It was a history that I wanted to relive and dreaded remembering. It was in those moments so long ago that I'd actually felt happy.

That I'd actually felt free.

Debbie seemed to be waiting for me to respond, so I offered her a smile and said, "Well, it's good to be back."

That seemed to appease her. She patted my hands once more before turning and walking away. Her voice trailed behind her as she spoke to whomever was on the other end of the phone call.

Alone again, I sat back on my chair. My appetite for these cookies had dissipated, and I resorted to picking the raisins from the one in front of me. Not wanting to sit here like a lonely old woman, I pushed myself out my chair and stood. Times like these called for fresh ocean air.

Luckily, I'd left my purse in my room, so as I left the inn, my hands and arms were free. I made my way down the porch stairs, and as soon as I made it across the parking lot and into the sand, I slipped my shoes off. I deposited them next to a bench and started making my way across the beach toward the ocean.

The roughness of the sand on the bottom of my feet uncovered so many faded memories. Coming here as a child. Spending time with my parents. I was happy here once. I had a good childhood here.

I just wish things had gone differently.

My parents always wanted me to go to school. To be something more than what they had been. That was probably why I pushed myself like I did. I wanted to prove that I wasn't going to make the same mistakes they had made.

When I met Roger, things changed. Suddenly, I wanted to see myself as a stay-at-home wife and mother. I was in love, and my parents couldn't handle that. There were a few times that they tried to break us up, but Roger and I never allowed it.

When I got pregnant with Maggie, we ran away. Roger took a job in New York, and I settled in, waiting for Maggie to be born.

But their influence never stopped. They infiltrated our lives. One day, when Maggie was a toddler, I realized that they were never going to stop. I was always going to be living with them behind me, pushing me to be who they wanted me to be.

When I left Roger, I knew it broke his heart. Leaving Maggie was the hardest thing I'd ever done. But I wasn't soft like Roger, and I knew she would be happier without me in her life.

I spent so much time telling myself that I didn't care that I started to believe it. It was easier to wrap myself up in my career than to face the daughter I'd left.

The daughter I'd hurt.

And now I was in danger of losing everything.

This time, when the tears pricked my eyes, I allowed them to flow. I was hurting, and I was tired of pretending like I was okay, because I wasn't. Sure, I was harsh and critical, but I'd learned that you never got anywhere by being a pushover. It was a cutthroat world out there, and that is what I wanted to teach my daughter.

I just never realized that I was going to regret it.

I stopped walking and turned to face the ocean. I wrapped my arms around my chest and stared out into the distance. The feeling of the salty air on my skin mixed with the tears that flowed down my cheeks made me feel…alive.

More alive that I'd been in a long time.

I closed my eyes and took deep breaths. Why was regret so heavy? Why did it feel as if I were breaking under its pressure? Was I ever going to feel whole again?

"Are you okay?"

For the third time that day, I was startled by someone approaching me. I quickly wiped at my cheeks and turned to see a woman standing there. She had a look of concern on her face as she studied me.

I sniffled and nodded. "I'm fine."

She didn't believe me. Instead, she waved for me to follow her. "Come with me. There's nothing that a little gelato can't fix. I'm just wrapping up for the day."

I glanced behind her to see a small rolling cart with the familiar logo of Mama Schmidt's on the side of it. I was instantly brought back to the gelato shack down the road. There were so many memories made on the picnic tables that lined the front of the shop. That seemed to be the theme of this trip: memories.

"Mama Schmidt's," I said with a reverence that must have tipped the woman off that I knew the place.

"Yeah, I own the shop." She glanced over at me. "Have you been to it?"

"Been to it? I had my first kiss right in front of the shop," I said waving in the direction of Mama Schmidt's.

She turned to me, her expression a mixture of laughter and surprise. "You did? No way."

I nodded. "Well before you were born."

"So you're a Magnolia native?"

"Born and raised."

"Then you knew my grandmother."

"Mama Schmidt?" I nodded. "Oh, yeah. I knew her. And she knew me." I had been a bit of a wild child on the island. To say that I had a reputation was an understatement.

"Fascinating," she said as she stepped up behind the cart and flipped open the cooler. "Well, what can I get you?"

I stared at the options in the cooler next to her. "Rocky road?"

"Made it fresh this morning."

"I'll take some of that."

She grinned as she grabbed a bowl and then peeled back the top of the tub. I watched her scoop a healthy heap and then scrape the scoop against the side of the bowl. Between the cookies I ate earlier and this gelato, I was going to have to spend the evening on the treadmill in the inn's new exercise room. If not, I was going to head home with wider hips than I'd come here with.

"Here you go," she said as she handed the creamy, cold goodness over.

I took it and slipped a spoonful into my mouth. It tasted like my teenage years. I moaned softly as I nodded. "Yep. Just as good as it was years ago."

I could see a sense of pride in her at my compliment.

"Thanks. I try to uphold the Schmidt name."

"Well, you succeeded. I'm sure your grandmother would be proud." I glanced down at the register and realized that I didn't have my money with me. "I don't have my wallet."

She laughed. "I figured from your lack of purse." She waved me away. "Don't worry about it. I'm sure if you knew my grandmother like you say you did, she would want you to have it."

A feeling of gratitude washed over me. Even though Evelyn Schmidt called me a hell'un, she would have offered any wanderer a scoop of gelato if they needed it. It was just the way she was.

"Name's Penny," I said as I reached my hand over the counter.

She took it. "Scarlett."

"It's nice to meet you."

"You too. It's good to have you back."

It was strange, but hearing those words, from the granddaughter of a woman who chased me away from her shop on numerous occasions, felt oddly satisfying. Like I'd been holding my breath until this moment. It was as if she were on the other side of the counter, smiling at me, telling me everything was forgiven.

My heart ached as I wished in that moment to return to a time when I could see Mama Schmidt again. When I could hug her and tell her that I was sorry.

Regret is a bitter pill that is only magnified when resolution is no longer in your reach. I just wished I'd learned that earlier and through less pain.

"You're Maggie's mom, right?"

Speaking of regrets... I nodded. "Does she talk about me?"

Scarlett shook her head. "Not really. But I think it's cool that you're here to help with the wedding. I'm sure it'll help fix whatever happened in the past." She fiddled with the spare change in the cup next to the register. "There's nothing a sorry and a bowl of gelato can't fix." She tapped her nose and then pointed at me. "Remember that."

That phrase. It was exactly what Mama Schmidt would have said to a customer. She was always dishing out advice along with her gelato. For a moment, it was as if she were standing there, doing the same for me.

Feeling too nostalgic for my taste, I just nodded as I grabbed a couple of napkins and turned to head back toward the inn. Scarlett called out a goodbye, and I waved my napkin-filled hand in her direction.

I tried to keep my mind clear as I made my way back. The ocean washed over my feet as I walked. The cool temperature helped ground me in the present when my mind wanted to wander to the past. To a time when my life felt so complicated. Looking back, I realized I had been mistaken. It had been simple. I just chose to see it through a different lens.

By the time I got back to my shoes and slipped my feet into them, I'd made a pact with myself. If I wanted my future to look different than my past, I needed to start thinking about what I wanted it to look like.

Was Maggie in it?

Yes.

Was my job in it?

Maybe.

Was I happy?

I hoped so.

FOUR

Fiona

I was crazy.

Completely and utterly crazy.

I groaned as I stared at the white house in front of me.

What was I doing here? Why had I woken up at six to get Blake ready to go to daycare, taken a shower, and packed a lunch like this guy was actually going to give me a job? Or like I was actually going to take it?

I leaned my forehead on the steering wheel and took in a few deep breaths. Breathing deep did nothing to calm my nerves. Instead, it made me feel light-headed and just as confused as before.

"You'll be fine. This will be fine. You'll just go in and clean his house and make his meals and then leave." I scoffed at myself. "People do this all the time, Fiona."

I waited, hoping my tone would change my mind…it didn't. I felt just as nervous, but now I also felt crazy.

I needed to get out of the car before anyone saw me talking to myself.

I gathered the cleaning supplies I grabbed from Mom's house. Then I twisted my hand around to grab the door release and pushed. Luckily, I got out of the car *and* slammed the door behind me without dropping anything.

That was a feat in and of itself.

I made my way around the house and toward the front door. With the sun rising in the sky, it made the place look less scary. In fact, the house had multiple windows where the blinds were closed, but I could tell if they were open, the light they would let in would be breathtaking. Especially with the oranges bleeding into the purples that streaked the sky.

I turned to stare at the ocean for a moment. How could someone so crabby live in a place that looked like paradise?

"You're late."

His deep voice startled me, and I screamed, throwing all of the bottles and rags into the air. I slammed my hand over my mouth as I turned to see him staring at the bottle of cleaner that was dangerously close to rolling off the edge of the deck. When I finally composed myself, I dropped down to gather my things.

"I'm sorry," was all I could muster. Great.

"I said eight sharp. It is now eight-oh-five. You're late."

I glanced up to see him standing there in a pair of

faded sweats and a grey T-shirt. His hair was floppy and covered half his face—the half that had the scar. My gaze lingered a bit too long, and suddenly, he was staring at me.

I quickly dropped my gaze and continued to pick up the rogue cleaning supplies. "It won't happen again."

"It better not."

Before I could respond—with something that I hoped would lighten the mood—Jackson turned and headed back into his house, swinging the door shut behind him. The word *wait* was poised on my lips, but I was never given the chance to get it out.

Instead, I stood there like an idiot all alone on his porch. I hurried to gather the rest of the supplies and shifted them, so my hand could freely turn the door handle. By the time I got inside, I wasn't sure where Jackson had wandered off to, but it wasn't the living room or kitchen.

This house was the epitome of open concept. Besides the stairs that led up to what I could only assume was a loft, there were no walls. The kitchen led into the dining room, and across from those spaces was the living room. There was a small closed-off room in the back that I could only assume was the bathroom.

I wondered what was upstairs, but then pushed that thought from my mind. If he wanted me up there, he would let me know. I busied myself with placing the bottles on the counter. I'd been right, the house was made of windows in the front. If he opened the blinds, the view would be spectacular.

I took a moment to take it in, and just as I turned to face the back of the house, my entire body froze. Jackson was at the top of the stairs. He was still wearing his faded sweats, but his shirt was no longer on his chest. Instead, it was draped over one shoulder. His tanned and very muscular chest made him look like a Greek god.

My entire body heated as I twisted around to stare at the blinds again. I closed my eyes, praying to get that image from my mind, but there was no way that was going to happen. Looking at Jackson's bare chest was like looking at the sun. It was burned into me.

"I eat eggs, bacon, and toast for breakfast," he said. His voice got louder, so I could only assume he was walking down the stairs. I kept my eyes pinched shut as I turned to nod.

"On it."

He was quiet, and I wasn't sure if he was still there or if he had left. I peeked through one slitted eyelid to find that, from what I could see, I was alone.

"What are you doing?"

I yelped as both eyes flew open. I turned to see him standing next to me. He had a glass of water in his hand, and he was eyeing me as he downed it in one gulp.

Watching him drink while half naked made my mouth run dry. Suddenly, I felt as if I were in the Sahara. "What do you mean?" I asked, my voice raspy and quiet.

"Why are you standing there with your eyes closed?"

I swallowed, but that didn't help. My mouth felt full of sawdust. "I was giving you privacy."

He frowned. "What?"

I blinked and then nodded toward his chest. When that didn't seem to register, I sighed and circled my hand around in front of him. "You looked like you were getting dressed, and I didn't want you to think that I was a Peeping Tom." My cheeks felt as if they were on fire by now. Why was he making me say this? Was he enjoying it?

Because I most certainly was not.

He watched me for a moment before he leaned closer. My heart rate picked up speed as he neared. I was fairly certain he could hear it. After all, it sounded like a megaphone in my own ears.

"If I wanted privacy, I wouldn't have come down here." He pulled back, drank the rest of his water, and tossed the cup into the sink. "You're my maid now. You're going to have to get used to seeing me like this."

I stared at him. The source of my tongue-tied reaction shifted quickly from shock to annoyance. Did he just say that to me? Before I could gather my thoughts, he was across the living room and closing the bathroom door behind him. I glared at the door as I blew out my breath.

Well, this was going to go just great.

Why did he have to be such a beast? I was already stressed out about Dave and the court, and now I had to deal with a grumpy employer as well. I was never going to complain about how Mom treated me ever again. Compared to Jackson, Mom was a marshmallow bunny.

I focused my attention on the dishes. Part of me wanted to waste the hot water just to stick it to him. If it ran out, that would be so sad…

I may have a problem.

Just as I was finished washing dishes and had moved to drying, the bathroom door opened. Even though I wanted to keep my attention forward, my gaze drifted in that direction.

A cloud of steam followed after him. Thankfully, Jackson was clothed in jeans and the T-shirt that he'd had slung over his shoulder. His hair was damp and hung in clumps around his head. His gaze was down as he walked back into the kitchen.

"No breakfast?" he asked as he pulled open the fridge.

I groaned. "I'm so sorry. I got distracted by the dishes. I wanted to clean the kitchen before I got started." *Plus, I wanted to waste the hot water.* I decided to keep that bit to myself.

Jackson made a sound in his throat that was similar to a growl. By the time I glanced back at him, he had a box of cereal out on the counter and, a moment later, a jug of milk next to it. He poured himself a heaping bowl, and after hc filled it to the brim with milk, he replaced the jug in the fridge and slammed the door.

I was too stunned to talk. After all, it wouldn't take me that long to make him breakfast. He *could* wait five minutes. "I was going to start as soon as I finished the dishes."

Jackson shook his head and shoveled a spoonful of cereal into his mouth. "I'm good. I'll just eat this." He avoided my gaze as he walked out of the kitchen and headed over to the living room to flip on the TV.

The sound of a sportscaster filled the air, and honestly, I was grateful that he was doing something other than staring at me or talking to me. With him distracted, I could work unimpeded.

I finished up the dishes and moved to giving the kitchen a deep clean. It seemed as if it hadn't been scrubbed in ages. Every so often, I glanced over at Jackson, wondering what his story was. Had he lived here long?

What was his connection with Maggie's mom? Did they know each other? It sure seemed that way last night. Penny was desperate for Jackson to do something, and he was adamant that he wasn't going to do it.

What was it that she wanted?

"You're staring."

I blinked, and my sight came into focus. I pulled back when I realized that Jackson's icy blue eyes were trained on me. He'd finished his cereal and was leaning back on the couch with his arm draped across the back.

"No, I wasn't."

Jackson snorted as he muted the commercial playing on the TV. "I could tell by the way your eyes were fixed on me. It's what we call 'staring' in the English language."

My cheeks were once again on fire. Why did this man irritate me so much? "Well, there is another term for it. Dazing off. Which is what I was doing."

"Or you were staring at me."

I narrowed my eyes at him and turned my back, returning my attention to his cupboards. "Maybe it's because we still haven't settled on how much you are paying me. Instead, you demand that I come inside, make you breakfast, and clean your house. And then you turn around and eat a bowl of cereal that is basically just puffed sugar."

"Do you want to make me breakfast?"

The nearness of Jackson's voice startled me. I yelped and turned so fast that the sponge I was using ricocheted across the room. My entire body felt as if it was going to burst into flames as our eyes followed the projectile.

Jackson was the first to return his gaze to me. "Jumpy much?"

It took a moment, but I was able to regain my composure enough to glare at him. "Well, if you keep appearing out of nowhere, I'm going to get a little freaked out." I held my ground as I peered up at him.

He was close. Too close.

He smelled like the woods after a summer rain— which was strange to say because I didn't think I'd ever been in the woods during a summer rain, but I was certain it would smell like he did now.

Whether it was his shampoo or his cologne, it smelled amazing. So much so that I wanted to lean in. Which I certainly couldn't do. Not when he was my boss. And definitely not when he was staring at me like he was trying to figure me out.

"You're staring at me," I whispered.

"It's called dazing off."

We stood there for a moment in silence. It was both calming and deafening at the same time. He was intense, that was for sure. The way his hair covered his left eye. The fact that under the curtain of hair was a scar. It all had my heart beating faster and my mind swirling. I wanted to know more about it.

I wanted to know more about him.

"You missed a spot," he said as he leaned in and then appeared again a moment later with an apple in hand. He took a large bite out of it and pointed at the counter.

I looked at what he was motioning to, but when I glanced back at where he'd been standing, he was gone. I found him once again on the couch with the volume on and the game resuming.

Now alone, I felt strange. What had happened there? Had he been flirting with me? Why did he constantly get close to me? Why did he look at me like he was trying to figure me out?

I swallowed, all of my emotions rising up into my throat and lodging themselves there. There was something seriously wrong with me.

Needing a break from the tense interaction between

us, I located the glass cleaner and paper towels and told him that I was heading out to clean the windows—but I doubted he even heard me. If he did, he didn't acknowledge me.

Once I got outside in the fresh air, I felt like I could breathe. The sun was warm on my skin as it beat down on me. I felt more alive out here than I ever felt in the coffee shop, even if my boss was a strange and eccentric man.

He definitely was different. But Penny trusted him, and Penny was Maggie's mom, so I could trust him. At least for now.

It took about an hour to clean the windows that I could reach. By the time I got back into the house, Jackson was gone. I peeked up at the loft and wondered if he was there but then directed my attention back to cleaning. I was fairly certain that maids didn't snoop. They got the job done and then left.

While cleaning the outside of the windows, I realized how dirty the inside panes were. My goal for today was to clean what I could reach inside, and tomorrow I'd make sure to grab a ladder from Jake. I was sure he'd have one I could borrow at the hardware store.

I opened all the blinds and was halfway through the windows when I heard a clattering noise. Before I could register what was happening, Jackson appeared next to me. He was frantically feeling for the lift cords and yanking the ones he could locate.

"What are you doing?" he asked. His voice was raw

and hoarse, and there was no way I could miss the panic in it.

"I'm cleaning the windows," I said as I stepped back, not sure why he was reacting this way.

"I never asked you to do that," he said, his back to me as he continued to close the blinds.

"It's my job. You told me to clean your house, so I'm cleaning your house."

Jackson was breathing so heavily that I could see his shoulders rise and fall. For some reason, he was more upset than I could ever imagine.

Were these special blinds? Had I touched something important and tainted it?

What was going on here?

"I'm sorry. I didn't realize that the windows were off limits. I won't do it again," I said as I raised my hands. I was still holding the bottle of window cleaner and a roll of paper towels.

"I think you should go," he said quietly.

I blinked. "What?"

"I said, I think you should go." He pushed away from the windows and passed by me. "This was a mistake."

"Because I opened your blinds?" I moved to follow him. He couldn't do this to me. I needed this job. "But I have a kid—"

"I said go." He had his hands firmly planted on the counter in front of him, and he was leaning forward, his hair covering his face.

There was no way I could catch his gaze. His body

language said there was no way we were talking about this. He'd spoken, and I was expected to obey.

"Are you firing me?" I hated that my voice came out in a squeak. I hated that I felt powerless. Every other aspect of my life was out of my control. This was the first thing that I had for myself, and I was losing it as well.

"Just go."

I had to stand there and watch him walk away. Yet another person in my life dictating how things were going to be and just expecting me to go along with it.

Not sure what to do, I left all the cleaning supplies on his counter and walked out. Sure, I'd let him win this fight today, but come tomorrow, I would be back.

He may have won the battle, but I was winning this war.

I had to.

FIVE

Penny

$\mathcal{I}$ felt happier when I woke up the next day. Well, happy was a strong word. I definitely felt more optimistic than I'd felt in a long time, and it was refreshing.

I wasn't getting anywhere with Jackson, but that was okay. I realized it was going to take time to break him down and get him to do what I wanted—and I was willing to wait. For now, I was going to spend time working on a past that I was determined to heal.

That started with Maggie.

If I focused on what I wanted in my future, perhaps it would give me the strength to fix my past.

I found her in the dining room when I got there at 7 a.m. She was busy filling the trays for the breakfast buffet, and she looked…happy. I almost didn't want to approach her. After all, I knew how she felt about me. I knew how broken I'd made her feel.

Could I fix my relationship with her? Was it selfish of me to ask that we strengthen the bond that I'd so readily cast aside?

Realizing that I might be approaching this in a way that only benefited me, I decided to take my time. I would work to ease myself back into her life. I would allow her to guide my actions.

Even though I loved being in control, I'd allow her to have the reins.

"Morning," I said as I grabbed a plate and stepped up to her.

Maggie startled and then glanced over at me. Her surprise turned to a smile when her gaze met mine. "Hey, morning."

The silence that fell between us felt strange. What was I supposed to say from here? I expected that she would have responded with a question or a statement, but we were still at the start of the conversation.

Since when had this gotten so hard?

I knew how to talk. I did it with strangers all the time.

Except, Maggie wasn't a stranger. She was my daughter, and I'd forgotten how to talk to her.

"What's the plan for today?" I finally managed as I filled my plate with eggs.

She returned the lid to a chafing dish and then turned to face me. "Archer and I are going to go pick invitations."

I grabbed the tongs and began to place some bacon

next to my eggs. "That sounds fun." In reality, it didn't, but I wasn't going to say that.

"Yeah…" She grew quiet. "Do you want to come with?"

I had a book to edit and emails to answer, but I was determined to start changing my life. If I truly meant that, I needed to start carving out time for my family. "What time?"

"Noon?"

I nodded. "I'll make that work."

Her smile widened. "Really?"

I hated how happy this made her. It only plunged the knife in my gut deeper. The knife that represented all my failures as a mom. If she was happy I was participating, that meant I'd failed her somewhere.

"I'm excited. It'll be good for you to spend more time with Archer as well. I want you two to get to know each other."

I smiled. "I'm excited too."

I'm not sure why my breakfast sat like a rock in my stomach, but it did. Maybe it was because I didn't normally eat food until noon. Or perhaps it was because I felt guilty. It made me wonder, could our relationship ever change? Or was this my life now?

After breakfast, I made my way up to my room and finished some work. By the time noon rolled around, I was stiff and ready to move. I slipped on my shoes and headed downstairs, where I found Maggie and Archer waiting for me.

Maggie gave me a soft smile, but Archer had a cooler demeanor with me. I wasn't sure why exactly, but I had a sinking feeling that he wasn't happy with me. I didn't blame him. I should have been there for Maggie more than I had been in the past. I'd dislike me too.

We climbed into Archer's truck, and we took off. The stationery place was across the bridge, and I found it relaxing to watch the scenery as it passed by. It was as beautiful as it was nostalgic. So many memories wrapped up in each place. It was strange to face what I'd run away from so long ago, with the life experience that I had now.

It was like seeing your past through a different lens.

"How does it feel to be back?"

I glanced toward the front to see Maggie peering over her shoulder at me. She looked so optimistic that it made me feel bad as my guilt resurfaced. Pushing those thoughts aside, I decided to focus on the present.

"Interesting. I haven't been here in so long that I thought it would feel different. But even though things look different, they are still familiar." I sighed. It felt like my words were coming out as a jumble of thoughts. I was slowly losing my mind.

Thankfully, Maggie didn't ask anymore soul-searching questions for the rest of the ride. Instead, she got a phone call from the baker and was distracted with cake questions. I took the time before we got to the store to clear my mind. There was no way I was going to survive this trip if I kept slipping down memory lane.

It wasn't good for my mental health.

Once Archer parked, we headed into the shop. A woman greeted us, and a moment later, we were looking at an arrangement of varying shades of off-white paper. I tried to feign interest, but I was too distracted to really give my opinion.

Maggie tried to include me, but I was no help. Instead, I just sat next to her, nodding along with everything she said. It was as if I were paralyzed to say anything. What would a good mother do? I didn't even know.

Did I push her? Or did I allow her to be who she was meant to be?

I thought I knew, but the longer I stayed in Magnolia the more I began to realize that I may have gotten it wrong. In my ignorance, I'd ruined my relationship with my daughter.

"You okay?" Maggie whispered after the millionth filigree option we were shown. Who knew that there were so many ways to draw a squiggly line?

I took a sip of the bottled water we'd been given. "I'm great. I just think I need some fresh air. Do you mind if I step out?"

Maggie glanced over at me, worry written across her features, but she didn't push me further. Instead she just nodded and waved toward the door.

I was out of my seat and across the room with a speed I hadn't achieved in ages. Once I was standing outside, I took in a few deep breaths. This was the second time in two days that I had to run from the room. There was something seriously wrong with me.

Thankfully, it took less time to gain control of my reaction, and soon, I was wandering down the street, looking through the shop windows. They were selling an assortment of trinkets, and when I discovered one was full of beads, I pulled open the door and slipped inside.

As a way to relax, I'd taken up jewelry making a few years ago. I wasn't amazing, but I was getting better with each piece.

I was studying a bead when the shop owner walked up behind me. "That's a beautiful piece."

I rolled it around in my fingers. "It is." It was Maggie's birthstone, peridot. I'd wanted to make her something, but never found the right items to do so. Plus, we didn't have the kind of relationship where I could just give her a gift, and I wasn't sure how to bridge the gap that I had created.

"It would look beautiful as a necklace or bracelet."

I studied the stone. She wasn't wrong. I wasn't sure if Maggie was a necklace or bracelet person, and it hurt that I didn't know that.

That was something a mother should know.

"I'll take it," I said as I picked up a few other beads as well as the materials to make her piece. I'd work hard to discover what she liked.

After my purchase, I headed back toward the stationery store. Maggie and Archer were waiting for me in the parking lot. Both of their gazes landed on my bag at the same time, and I couldn't help but see the disappointment in Maggie's eyes.

Archer didn't hide his frustration with me. He just scoffed and rounded the car. "Come on, let's go," he said to Maggie.

As much as I wanted to explain myself, I realized that I'd been the reason for my poor relationship with Maggie, and any excuse would just sound hollow. All I could do was offer Maggie a weak smile as we both climbed into the back of the truck and Archer started up the engine.

The ride back to Magnolia was quiet, which I was grateful for. If Maggie had tried to talk, I wasn't even sure what I would say. When we were quiet, I could think. I could sort through my thoughts and plan my words.

It was the time I needed to compose myself.

Archer pulled into the inn, and Maggie got out. Apparently, Brett had texted her an SOS, and she was out the door before the engine was even off. I moved to pull on the handle but stopped when Archer spoke.

"Listen, we both know you are here for whatever is going on with your author and then you are going to leave again." His voice was quiet, and his focus was forward as if he were carefully calculating his words.

I parted my lips to speak but then slowly closed them. I didn't want to give him excuses. From what I could tell of Archer, he was good at reading people. There was no way I was going to be able to convince him otherwise.

And, honestly, my actions would speak louder than words. If I wanted to change his mind, he was going to need to see proof.

"If you're going to leave and never come back, just stop what you're doing right now." He slowly turned to face me. "So I'm not the one picking up the broken pieces of her heart."

I could see the anguish in his gaze. It was the look of a man who had to watch the woman he loved cry while being completely unable to stop it.

I was the reason she cried.

"I'm sorry," I whispered, my words catching in my throat.

He studied me for a moment before he sighed. "Those are words your daughter needs to hear, not me."

I nodded. "Of course."

He paused before he pulled open his door. Then he was gone, and I was alone, staring at his retreating frame.

A sob escaped my lips as all the regret I'd been pushing down rose to the surface. What had I done? Had I really made life that bad for her?

Was there a chance of coming back?

Could we pick up the pieces?

I crumpled the bag of beads and shoved it into my purse. In my attempt to make amends, I'd just made things worse. Again.

After getting to my room, I took a hot shower, crawled into my pajamas, and slipped into bed. With the latest Hallmark movie playing on the TV, I dove into the bag of M&Ms that I'd bought at a gas station in Connecticut.

At one point, I shot Jackson a text, but it went unanswered. Just like all the previous ones.

Feeling rejected and broken, I snuggled under my blankets and sighed. If this was the worst that things were going to get, then I guessed I was pretty lucky even if I felt like crap.

Things that were broken down could be built back up. I was still determined to make the necessary changes to make that happen.

I'd be that person for Maggie, and hopefully, I could figure out what Jackson needed.

I needed the win. I needed something positive to happen, and I needed it fast.

I was about to lose the life I'd built for myself and my daughter in one swoop if I didn't work hard to save both. Tomorrow, after a good night's sleep, I was going to wake up and start again. Every day brought new opportunities to be the person I was meant to be.

Every day brought a do-over.

And lately, I was in desperate need of those.

Fiona

___

*S*tanding in front of Jackson's door the next morning, I officially declared myself crazy. Only a crazy person would return to the home of a man who literally kicked them out the day before.

I may have been a glutton for punishment, but I wasn't ready to give up just yet. I would force him to give me a second chance. After all, that was what a decent human being did. They gave second chances.

I knocked on the door three times and then waited.

When no one responded, I knocked again.

Nothing.

I tried to peek through the windows, but Captain Blinds had the place boarded up. There was no way anyone was going to see inside. If I didn't know the state of the house or the fact that a person lived there, I would have assumed the place was condemned.

I returned to the door and knocked again. "I know you're in there. It's not like you leave."

I squinted through the sunlight that reflected off the glass in hopes that I would see some movement. Thankfully, before I had to shout out at him once more, the door opened a crack, so he could barely see out.

"I told you not to come."

I put on my best desperate face. "I left my supplies. I'm here to get them and pick up my check."

The door opened a bit more. "Check?"

I nodded. "I worked for four hours yesterday, and you need to pay me."

"I'm not paying you."

"Then I'll report you."

He frowned. "To who?"

I stopped to think. "The Department of Labor?"

He scoffed. "I doubt that."

"Come on, be a nice guy, and pay me. Plus, let me get my stuff."

Jackson studied me for a moment before he sighed and pushed the door open. "Only for a minute."

I stepped inside, silently cheering my success. The first step was to get into his house, which I'd accomplished. The second step was convincing him that he needed me.

He left to disappear upstairs, and I took the time alone to open his fridge and pull out his eggs and bacon. I had both sizzling on the stove when he came back.

"What are you doing?" he asked as he descended the stairs.

I stepped back from the stove, so I could flip the eggs. "I'm making you breakfast."

"I'm not paying you for that."

I shrugged. "Maybe if you taste my food, it'll change your mind."

Jackson narrowed his eyes, but I could tell that the smell was tempting him. There was a desire in his expression as his gaze swept the stove. "I'm not promising anything."

"I understand. Just give me a chance"

He sighed, headed over toward the small table in the far corner of the kitchen, and plopped down. "Fine."

Butterflies erupted in my stomach as I busied myself. With the bacon sitting on some paper towels and the eggs steaming on his plate, I focused on perfectly toasting two pieces of bread. After I buttered them, I plated the food and set it in front of him.

He leaned forward, inspecting the food as if I'd hidden something there. Then he dove in. It didn't take long before the entire plate was clean, and Jackson was licking the last remnants of egg from his fork. He set it down and leaned back. His gaze was focused on me as he narrowed his eyes.

I hated that I cared so much about what he thought. I'd just met the man, after all. Despite what my mind told me, the anxiety in my chest said otherwise. I wanted the praise.

He pushed away from the table and stood. Then he stepped up next to me—a stance I was beginning to learn was a part of who he was. He didn't shy away from personal space. He took charge of it.

"Promise you will never open the blinds again?"

I swallowed as I took in his intense stare. I nodded. "I won't do that again."

"Promise to be on time?"

I nodded again.

He studied me. "Promise to make me eggs like that again?"

"Yes."

He lifted a check in front of me. It was made out for one hundred dollars. "This is half your daily salary. If you keep to those three promises, then I will pay you two hundred dollars a day, six days a week."

I parted my lips. Partly from shock at the number. My brain panicked over what he'd just said. But before I spoke, his gaze drifted down to my mouth and then back up to meet my gaze, completely distracting me.

"Is that going to be a problem?" he asked.

I blinked a few times, which helped clear my head. Once I could wrap my brain around what I was going to say, I cleared my throat. "I…"

Wait. How much did I want him to know about my life? Did I tell him about Blake? What would he say? Was it too much? I thought him not caring would hurt more than him being indifferent.

Jackson wanted an answer. He wanted to know why I was so hesitant.

So I decided not to hold back. After all, if I was going to work here nearly every day, he was going to find out. "I have a son."

He must have not anticipated that response. I watched his expression turn from intrigue to confusion. He took a step back. "A son?"

I nodded. "I want to see him on the weekends. Especially if I'm going to be here so much during the week."

He cleared his throat as he glanced around. Then he peered back at me. "You can bring him here."

I laughed. I didn't mean to, but this wasn't a kid-friendly house. I covered my mouth with my hand. "I'm sorry. I just don't think that Blake and fancy furniture would really jive."

Jackson shrugged. "I'm not attached to this stuff. It came with the house."

So that explained the dust and the matronly decorations. "Oh."

"So you'll bring him on Saturdays?"

I didn't like making this deal. I didn't like the idea of introducing Blake to any guy—even if he was only my boss. There were boundaries that I'd set for myself, and I didn't want to cross them. But I could use the extra money. At least for now. And really, what would it hurt? I'd bring Blake's tablet, and he'd be set for a few hours. Despite the warning bells sounding in my mind, I took in a deep breath and said, "Sure," as I blew that breath out.

He clapped his hands, and for the first time since I'd met him, I saw a spark of happiness flash across his face before it disappeared. "We have a deal," he said as he extended his hand.

I was fairly certain that this wasn't how the hiring process usually went, but if this was what he wanted, I was willing to go along with it. After all, he was the one paying me. I reached out and grabbed his hand.

His handshake was firm and surprisingly warm. I guess I figured with his recluse attitude he might be some sort of cold-blooded vampire. But Jackson's hand was big and warm. I could feel the calluses on his palm, but not in a bad way. In fact, it sent a shock of warmth throughout my body as my gaze drifted down to our hands.

Suddenly feeling vulnerable, I pulled my hand back and clasped it in front of me. I was going to ignore whatever had just happened. I *finally* had something good going for me, and I wasn't going to mess it up now.

Ready to get to work, I motioned toward the kitchen and offered Jackson a small smile. "Well, I should get to work. No time like the present."

Jackson watched me for a moment before he nodded and wandered over to the living room.

I worked in silence until the kitchen was clean. I took my time wiping down the tops of the cupboards and removing the dishes from the shelves and dusting them off. It felt good to clean. I needed that kind of win in my life. I'd spent so long feeling as if I couldn't control what was happening to me, but with cleaning, I could take charge.

I knew if I worked hard, I'd end up with a clean, sparkling space.

"I've never seen someone look so content when they're cleaning," Jackson murmured as I walked into the living room and started to remove the knickknacks from the bookshelf. He was sprawled out on the couch and staring at the screen in front of him.

"I look content?" I asked as I pressed my hands to my cheeks.

Jackson didn't respond right away, and his silence surprised me. He didn't seem like the kind of guy who got rattled easily—unless I was opening his blinds.

"I can tell by the way your body is relaxed." He spoke so quietly that I had to lean forward to catch what he'd said.

"Relaxed?" I asked as I rolled my shoulders. It was strange that Jackson noticed that. He wasn't wrong, but we'd only just met yesterday, and he was talking like he knew me.

Like he knew my tells.

"Well, I'm not wrong, am I?"

I moved a large globe down to the floor, shook out my rag, and started wiping the shelf I'd just cleared. "You aren't wrong."

He was quiet. I peeked over at him and allowed myself to wonder what his story was. Why was he here? How did he afford things when I never saw him work?

"So what makes you happy?" I asked, deciding to go the less direct route. I figured it would be easier to lead the conversation in the direction I wanted it to go if I didn't start out with, "So, *are you a trust-fund baby?*"

"What makes me happy?"

I nodded.

"Being alone." His voice was quiet and deep. I could hear the emotion as he spoke, which surprised me. If you just listened to the words, you would think he was being sarcastic. But the sincerity I heard in his voice changed things.

He really preferred to be alone.

The meaning of that statement made me sad. Who wanted to be alone? Why did that make him happy?

"Why?" The question was out of my lips before I could stop it. As soon as I spoke, I wanted to take it back. It wasn't my place to prod him. But there was something inside of me, something deep down, that wanted to know.

He was a good-looking guy, and judging from his ability to purchase this house and not work, he seemed well-off. What was he running from that made him want to stay alone in a house with the windows covered up?

Jackson never answered my question. Instead, he stood up and wandered to the fridge, pulled out a Coke and popped the top.

"So what's your son's name?"

I eyed him. Did he really care, or was he asking me as a way to change the subject? He probably just didn't want to spill his guts to his housekeeper, so I went along with his question.

"Blake."

"Ah. And he's how old?"

"He'll be four at the end of the year." My heart ached. I missed my baby. He was all I had right now, and I wasn't spending time with him. I was trying to tell myself it was because we needed this job. The money was going to pay for the basic things that I hadn't been able to provide for a long time.

It was hard to be both mom and provider, and I was determined to make the best of it. But it wasn't easy. I was beginning to realize that I was never going to make it out of motherhood without some scars and bruises. But Blake and I would be the better for it.

"And his dad?"

The mention of Dave had heat pricking the back of my neck. I turned to focus on the bookshelf I'd been dusting. I could hear Jackson return to the couch behind me. I wanted to respond to his question, but there were so many emotions erupting at the mention of my ex, and I wasn't sure I was ready to reveal them to a stranger.

"Not in the picture." There, that was basic enough and certainly didn't encourage more questions.

"I'm sorry."

His response startled me. That was the most genuine thing he'd said to me since I'd met him. I normally hated that response—after all, why was he sorry? It wasn't like it was his fault or anything.

Even though it annoyed me, I enjoyed seeing the more human side of Jackson. It was refreshing and made him appear less threatening.

"Thanks. It's just Blake and me and Mom now." I smiled at the thought of my small family. I moved to clean the next shelf and sneezed as the dust rose up and tickled my nose.

"Your mom? Does she live close?"

I glanced over my shoulder. Jackson was certainly chatty. I wouldn't have pegged him as much of a talker. "Yeah. She runs the local coffee shop. We moved in with her after we left Nashville."

"Nashville? What were you doing there?"

"My ex wanted to be a singer. So I followed him there. Big mistake." I turned to face Jackson now. I swung the dusting rag around as I spoke. As the last words left my lips, I realized what I'd done. I'd wanted to keep my life a secret, and yet here I was, spilling my guts a moment later.

What type of magic was this?

"I've been to Nashville. It's nice. Have I heard of your ex?"

Now he was continuing as if he hadn't just intruded on my past. I pinched my lips together. "Do you do this often?"

He glanced over at me with a genuinely surprised look on his face. "Do what?"

"Finagle people's personal information from them." I narrowed my eyes. "Are you a con artist?"

He paused for a moment before he let out a laugh. It was deep and meaningful. Like he hadn't laughed in ages and the sound had been building inside of him, wanting to be released. "A con artist? Is that what you think I do?"

I shrugged. "I wouldn't rule it out. You live alone. You're rich. You have scars..." The last statement lingered in the air. I pinched my lips. I hadn't really meant to say it. I monitored Jackson's reaction, hoping that I hadn't overstepped.

"Interesting. Is that what the town is saying?"

So he was just going to blow past it. I took that as a good sign. He wasn't as bothered by the fact that I'd seen his scar as he'd been the first time we met. Did that mean we were becoming friends? Did he see me as someone he could confide in?

"I'm not sure. I'm either with Blake, the coffee shop, or here." I tapped my chin. "I do hang out with some of the ladies in town, but we haven't gotten together in a while." I sighed when I realized how pathetic I sounded. "What I'm trying to say is, I'm a loser that has no friends."

He clicked his tongue. "I doubt that you are a loser."

"Oh really?" I snorted. "You must be blind then because I'm definitely not who I used to be."

Jackson fell quiet, and his features stilled. He turned his soda around in his hands a few times before he took a drink and then set it down on the coffee table in front of him. The tension between us had returned, which confused me.

What had I said? I ran through my response in my mind a few times and came up empty-handed each time. I'd spent every word insulting myself. Why would he take offense to that?

"What I'm trying to say is that I'm not sure what the town is saying, but you have to assume that they are saying something. I mean, a mysterious and sexy newcomer moves into town and holes up in his house, never coming out." I clicked my tongue. "If you don't want them to talk, you should get out more."

He was quiet for a moment before his smile returned. "You think I'm sexy?"

Heat permeated my cheeks once more. I turned quickly away from him, so he couldn't see how flustered that made me. I focused on wiping down the entertainment center that held his obviously new TV. The entire time, I could hear him chuckling. It wasn't until his phone rang that he stopped.

"Hello?"

I closed my eyes, not believing that I'd said that. I was an even bigger loser than I'd let on. I needed to keep my mouth shut. Like, locked up, sealed tight, throw away the key type of closed.

"Yeah, I'm here. I'm with my housekeeper who thinks I'm sexy."

Great. I was never going to live it down.

"Sure. Get me some sweet and sour chicken. Okay. See you tonight."

He hung up the phone and set it down on the coffee

table. Then he leaned back with his arm once again draped across the back of the couch. He looked pleased with himself as he focused on the game he was watching.

"Hot date?" I asked, hoping we could move past my ridiculous blunder.

He flicked his gaze over to me. "Would that make you jealous?"

I groaned and gathered my cleaning supplies as I headed toward the kitchen. "Absolutely not."

He nodded. "Good. 'Cause it's just my buddy coming over to watch a game."

"Great. Sounds like a great use of time."

He chuckled once more before he focused back on the TV.

I hurried out of his way, and once I'd set the supplies down on the counter, I blew out my breath. I shouldn't have revealed so much to Jackson, and I certainly never should have told him I thought he was sexy.

Or asked if he had a hot date.

And I certainly shouldn't have felt relieved when he said he didn't.

That was my biggest mistake of the afternoon.

SEVEN

Penny

$\mathcal{I}$ woke up the next morning feeling a little bit more optimistic than I had when I went to bed. My conversation with Archer was still reeling in my mind, but I was trying hard not to take offense at what he said. After all, he loved my daughter. He just wanted to protect her, which only made me like him more.

He was protective, and that was more than Sean had ever been for her.

Even though I'd been MIA for most of Maggie's first marriage, I knew she hadn't been happy. When I discovered that she was divorcing him, I was shocked. She wasn't the type to give up easily. The more I thought about it, the more I began to realize that I trusted Maggie. I knew she wasn't a rash person.

If he wasn't good, he wasn't good, and I didn't need to question that.

Even though I had a hard time showing that to

Maggie, it was truly how I felt, and I wanted her to know that.

Yet another way I'd failed my daughter and another thing I needed to repent of.

My list was getting longer and longer.

After a shower, I got dressed and styled my hair in a low bun. Then I applied a little bit of makeup, found my shoes, and headed out of the room. I wasn't sure what I was going to do today. I texted Jackson, but he, yet again, wasn't answering, so I pushed that from my mind.

I'd stop by his place tomorrow, but for now, I was going to focus on the people who weren't currently shutting me out of their life. Those who wanted me around.

Maggie was nowhere to be found by the time I walked into the dining room. It was abuzz with people dishing up their breakfasts and talking. I quickly made a plate and hurried to the corner of the room where I sat down and began eating.

Everyone looked at ease, and the serving tables were meticulously taken care of, so I knew Maggie wasn't far. She would be back any minute, and I could tell her good morning when I saw her.

Just as my coffee was cool enough to drink, Maggie's friend Clementine walked into the room. She scanned the tables, and I tried to look busy, but that didn't dissuade her. I wanted to keep out of Maggie's life here as much as possible. I didn't want her to feel like I was intruding on her space.

That meant creating definite lines between me and her friends.

My indifference didn't seem to affect Clementine. She made a beeline for my table and plopped down on the seat next to me. She gave me a wide smile as she leaned back.

"Good morning," she said as she reached forward and grabbed a wrapped chocolate from the middle of the table. She settled back and began to unwrap it.

"Good morning." I took a sip of my coffee.

Clementine popped the chocolate into her mouth as she glanced around. "Maggie here?"

"I haven't seen her."

Clementine sighed. "Bummer. I was hoping to catch her before things got too busy." She nodded in the direction of the full tables. "Apparently, I grossly misjudged how popular this place has become."

I nodded. Maggie had shown me the inn's numbers, and she was just booming. Most of her rooms were booked on the weekends, and there was a steady stream of people who stayed throughout the week. With all the improvements she and Archer had been making, they had turned this place into a viable business.

Putting my dollars into my daughter had been the best decision I'd ever made. Especially if I was in danger of losing my own livelihood.

"I wanted to talk to her about our next read for the book club."

My forkful of eggs was already midway to my lips,

but I paused at this news. I went ahead and slipped it into my mouth. I focused back on Clementine. "Book club?"

She nodded as she scrunched the chocolate wrapper between her fingers. "When we were cleaning the attic here, we discovered a photo of her grandmother and a group of women on the island. They started the Red Stiletto—"

"Book Club," I finished. My heart squeezed at the mention of the group. I remembered my mother starting it. She had been so excited when she came up with the name. "I know."

Clementine nodded. "That's right. My mom and your mom were a part of it." She sighed. A small smile tugged at her lips as if she were reliving a good memory.

I felt jealous. Why didn't I feel that way when I remembered my mother? Why did I let things get hard and then stay that way? I shook my head slightly, pushing those thoughts from my mind. I wasn't going to focus on the past anymore. All that mattered was what I did with the future.

"That's exciting that you restarted it."

Clementine nodded. "Yeah. We try to talk about books when we get together, but most times we just end up drinking and eating." She leaned closer to me. "It's more fun that way."

"I bet."

Clementine tapped her fingers on the table and sighed. "Without Maggie's help, I guess I'm alone in picking our next read." Then she paused and glanced in my direction. "Unless you want to help. I mean, you are an editor. Maybe you can share your favorite book?"

My mind started to race. A familiar reaction that happened every time someone wanted to talk about books or writing. It was my passion and my love, but my job had sucked some of that out of me. Dealing with the bureaucracy of publishing was not as exciting as discovering a story unfolding on the page.

I had a new book coming out. Perhaps if Jackson saw the public's reaction to his book, he would be more willing to come out of the den he'd created, and I could finally get out of the hot water I was in.

It really was a win-win-win situation.

"I love that idea."

Clementine looked genuinely surprised. Then she tapped the table. "Great. We can stop by the library and look through the selection."

I shook my head. "I have a better idea."

CLEMENTINE LOOKED surprised when I told her my book club pick involved a call to my office. Three rings and Harper answered. I explained that I needed ten books sent to Magnolia. I half expected her to tell me no, but I was pleasantly surprised when she quickly agreed to overnight them.

With that out of the way, I tucked my phone into my purse and turned my attention to Clementine. "It's a new release that no one has seen before." I leaned in. "You're getting an exclusive look."

She raised an eyebrow. "Wow. That's big."

I smiled at her. If she only knew. Jackson was a master with the written word. I still couldn't understand why he was being like this. After all, he'd won awards. He was my highest paid author. People stood in line for hours just to buy his book on release day.

To give that up boggled my mind.

His gift needed to be shared with the world.

Clementine seemed satisfied with what had just transpired. Just as she moved to stand, I reached out to stop her.

"I was wondering..."

She settled back in her seat.

I gave her a soft smile. "I was wondering if you could show me around town. It's changed a lot since I've been here. Plus, I'm worried I'm becoming a bother to Maggie." I patted her hand. "You know, one Magnolian to another."

Clementine paused before she glanced down at her watch. Then she slowly nodded. "Yeah, I think I can do that." She smiled at me. "That would be fun."

I set my fork down. "Really?" I asked as I pushed out my chair and grabbed my purse.

"Of course. We just have to stop by the hardware store, and then we can do whatever you want."

"Great."

I followed behind her as she led me from the room.

Just as we entered the foyer, Maggie looked up from behind the reception desk.

"Hey, Clem. Penny?" She furrowed her brow. "Where are you two going?"

"Mags, your mom hooked us up for the next book club meeting." Clementine jutted her thumb in my direction. "It's apparently a brand-new book. We're getting an exclusive preview."

Maggie raised her eyebrows. "Wow. That's great, Penny."

"Plus, that means we don't have to figure it out ourselves."

Maggie nodded. "So are you on your way to pick up the books?"

Clementine shook her head. "Naw, those are being shipped. I'm taking your mom out for the afternoon. She wants to see Magnolia, and since you're so busy..." Clementine shrugged as she motioned toward the inn.

Maggie nodded again. "Oh, okay. Well, have fun."

"Unless you want me here." I couldn't help but notice that she seemed a little disappointed by what Clementine had said.

"No, no, go. It'll be good for you to get out, and I can't leave. Not when we're bursting at the seams."

I thought about telling her I'd stay, but I also didn't want to bother her. If I was sticking around, she would feel like she needed to entertain me, and I didn't want that. Space was exactly what I would have wanted from my mom. I couldn't forget that.

"I'll be back tonight, and we can do dinner together?" I offered.

Maggie picked up the ringing phone and placed the call on hold. Then she turned her attention to me. "Really, it's fine. Have fun and don't worry about being back at a certain time."

I tried not to let her words get to me. It was an emotional roller coaster trying to mend a relationship. It was as if we were walking on eggshells, never knowing if we'd offended the other. Never knowing if they meant what they said or if there was a deeper meaning hidden between the words.

It was enough to make you feel as if you were going crazy.

Maggie returned to the call, so I followed Clementine out of the inn and over to her car. Thankfully, Clementine kept the conversation easy, asking me about my job and which authors I worked with.

I was happy to talk about my career. After all, it was such a huge part of my life. I lived and breathed it.

When we got to the hardware store, I got out and followed Clementine. I remembered coming here with my father, and it filled me with nostalgia to walk through the doors once more.

"Wow," I whispered as I glanced around. "It's exactly the same."

"What?" Clementine asked, her voice rising an octave. "It's not exactly the same. I moved the hammers to aisle seven instead of five." She wiggled her eyebrows. "Big changes are always happening here."

I chuckled. As soon as Jake approached her and pulled her in for a kiss, I wandered away. It wasn't that kissing made me feel uncomfortable; it was just that I hadn't been in a relationship for so long that it was strange to be around it.

The publishing world was cutthroat. No one had time for relationships, and if you did find someone who put up with your crazy hours and late-night phone calls, people saw it as a weakness.

You were less likely to get authors assigned to you. After all, how could you leave at the last minute to fly to Europe for a book tour? It was better to stay detached than to find someone who would love you enough to stick around through all of that.

So when I found myself around people in love, it was best for me to wander away than to confront the life I'd always wanted but never allowed myself to have.

A few minutes later, after staring at electrical material like I knew what I was looking at, I found myself standing in front of a little shop. There was no glass in the space, instead, a small counter jutted out. All sorts of mechanical things were set on top with little white tags affixed to them.

The sign *Spencer's Corner* was hung above the window, and a small bell with the sign *ring for service* sat propped next to it. I contemplated ringing the bell, but then pushed that thought from my mind. I was certain that whoever Spencer was, he was busy and wouldn't appreciate being bothered like this.

Still, I ran my fingers against the cold metal of the bell as I studied the machine parts next to it. Mechanical things fascinated me. Maggie's father was a mechanic, and he was always tinkering with different things. Being here caused memories to emerge that I thought had disappeared forever. It both excited and scared me.

"Did you need something?" a deep, grating voice asked.

I glanced up and jerked my hand away, knocking a few things onto the ground at the same time. I caught a glimpse of my questioner before I bent down to pick up the little trinkets that I'd knocked over.

He was an older man, wearing a white shirt covered with grease and sporting a bushy beard. He had a scowl on his face, so I took my time to collect the items. I was definitely not welcome here.

"I'm so sorry," I said as I set the items down on the counter. "I'm just waiting for Clementine to finish up." I held up my hands. "I have nothing to drop off."

The man—whom I could only assume was Spencer—picked up the things I'd set down and put them on a counter behind him. "Why were you going to ring the bell?" he asked as he pointed in the bell's direction.

"I wasn't. I was just…" I swallowed as I forced the next words out. "Playing with it."

My cheeks burned. That response made me sound like a child.

"Playing with it?"

I nodded. "I'm sorry. I'm sure you are busy, and I didn't mean to bother you." I smoothed my hair down as I backed up toward the aisles.

Thankfully, he didn't follow, and a moment later, I found myself standing next to Clementine and Jake, who were deep in conversation. I didn't want to be rude, but I also didn't want to linger here. Not when I'd made such a fool of myself.

"Ready to go?" I asked, offering Clementine a big smile. One that I hoped would hurry her along.

She nodded and kissed Jake goodbye, and we walked out together. Once we were in her car and pulling out of the parking spot, I decided now was the best time to bring up Spencer.

I was fairly certain that there was no way I was going to be able to forget him. He was handsome and brooding and most likely bad for me. All the ingredients needed for the perfect man.

"I met Spencer," I said casually.

Clementine glanced over at me. "You did?" She pushed the car into drive. "What did you think?"

"He was nice."

"Yeah. He's interesting. Dad hired him years ago. He likes to keep to himself."

I nodded. "So it's just him?" I winced. Was that too forward?

Probably. After all, it wasn't like I was going to make Magnolia my home, and while I was here, I needed to work on Jackson and Maggie. I didn't have time in my life for a mysterious man who most likely had just showed up in my path to break my heart.

If I was wise, I would end this conversation and force myself to never think of him again.

But I wasn't wise.

Not in the slightest.

"You want to know about Spencer?"

I shrugged and settled back. I'd gone this far, I might as well keep going. "Tell me all the dirt."

Clementine laughed. "I'm not sure that there's a lot of dirt, but I can tell you what I know."

I smiled. "Sure. Let's start there."

EIGHT

Fiona

hankfully, when I got home from Jackson's house, I was so busy that I only thought about him a total of ten times. Compared to how discombobulated I felt while I was with him, I counted that as a win.

My night was filled with a long conversation with Austin about our plan of attack for the court date in three weeks punctuated by a screaming Blake. He was running a low-grade fever, and that resulted in a cranky, hard-to-get-to-sleep child.

I gave him a cool bath and some fever reducer, and then I snuggled with him in bed until he fell asleep.

It wasn't until I woke up at one in the morning with a crick in my neck and my clothes still on that I realized I'd fallen asleep in bed with him. My mouth felt like something had died in it, and my stomach growled. In the craziness of the evening, I'd forgotten to eat. Again.

I felt Blake's forehead, and it felt cooler. His fever had

broken. I blew out a sigh of relief. That meant I wouldn't have to keep him from preschool today. Which meant I could go to Jackson's house and work.

Jackson.

I stifled a groan as my thoughts returned to his dark blue eyes and brooding demeanor. What was I doing? Why was I thinking about him in any capacity other than my boss? After all, I'd held many jobs, and never in my life had my employer infiltrated my thoughts as much as Jackson did.

There was something seriously wrong with me.

After sneaking my arm out from under Blake, I placed both feet on the floor and tiptoed from the room. Mom was asleep, so the apartment was dark. When I got to the kitchen, I flipped on the light. I squinted as I glanced around.

I wasn't sure what to eat, but I didn't have much energy to start cooking. Just as I pulled out a pan for some ramen, my phone rang. I slipped it from my pocket and glanced down, confused as to who might be calling me this late.

Jackson.

My heart galloped in my chest as I peeked quickly at the clock just to make sure I wasn't somehow dreaming. The red numbers on the oven read, 1:37.

My attention went back down to my phone, and I slid the green button across my screen. "Hello?" I asked.

"Fiona?"

"Yeah." If this was a dream, it was a strange one.

"It's Jackson. I was wondering…" He took in a deep breath. "I cut myself, and I'm bleeding. Any chance you can come help me?"

I furrowed my brow. Had I heard him right? He was *bleeding*, and he'd called me? "Is it bad?"

"Yeah."

"Can you call an ambulance?" I wasn't a stranger to blood. There were many nights I'd spent fixing up Dave's face after he got into a fight. But if the cut was deep enough for him to be calling me about it, why wasn't he going to a hospital?

When Jackson didn't respond right away, I glanced down at my phone just to make sure we hadn't been disconnected. The timer was still ticking up, so that wasn't the reason for his silence.

"I mean, if you need help, I would think that's where you'd want to go first."

"I don't do hospitals." His voice was low and curt.

"Oh." What was I supposed to say to that? If he didn't like them, then what could I do to convince him to go? That left me with two choices—neither of which I was too fond of. Either I let my employer bleed out, or I climb into my car and head over there to help.

If I wanted the money from my job, I figured the best thing for me to do was make sure the person writing the checks was still alive to do so.

"I'll leave right now," I said as I shouldered my purse and pulled my keys out.

Jackson muttered, "Thank you," and hung up. I

slipped on my shoes and then made my way over to Mom's room. I woke her up to let her know that I was leaving and would be right back. She was groggy but got up and shuffled into my room, where she collapsed on the bed next to Blake.

With my son taken care of, I slipped on my light jacket and headed out of the apartment.

With no traffic, the drive to Jackson's house was quick, and before I knew it, I was throwing the car into park and climbing out. I didn't knock this time when I got to the door. I just opened it and let myself in.

The house was dark, except for a single light in the kitchen. Jackson was standing next to the sink with a towel pressed to his hand. He looked pale, and when his gaze met mine, I could see the pain inside of it.

He was hurting.

I dropped my purse at the door and kicked off my shoes. I grabbed a dining room chair as I passed by and brought it over to him.

"Sit," I ordered as I turned the kitchen faucet on to allow the water to warm. "Where's you first aid kit?"

Jackson tipped his head forward while he rested his arm on the counter next to the sink. "Bathroom. Upstairs."

I started making my way toward the stairs before I paused. He'd made it fairly clear that he didn't want me going up there for any reason. Even though he'd just directed me to go up there, there was a part of me that wanted to verify he was okay with this.

"It's fine," he moaned.

I nodded and hurried upstairs.

The loft was tidy. There was a king bed along the far wall, with a large window above it. It was pitch black now, but I could tell that during the day, the view was spectacular. Besides the bed, there was a nightstand, dresser, and desk. A computer sat on top of the desk, but that was it. Nothing to indicate how he made his money.

There was a small bathroom to the left of where I stood. It didn't take long for me to find the small box in the bottom of the vanity with a red cross on it. I grabbed it and stood, making my way down the stairs with the box tucked under my arm.

Jackson's eyes were closed as he rested his head on his outstretched arm. I dragged another chair over to him. That woke him up. He straightened and glanced over at me as I gingerly brought his hand to my lap, so I could get a closer look at what I was dealing with.

"What did you do?" I asked as I unwrapped his finger, revealing the cut. It was deep, but it didn't go to the bone and, from what I could tell, could heal on its own. I would just need to clean it so that it didn't get an infection.

"I was cutting an apple," he said. His voice was quiet, and I could feel his gaze on me as he watched me.

I cleaned the cut with some hydrogen peroxide and dabbed it gently. I brought my gaze up to gauge his reaction. That way, I would know how much pressure I could put on the cut. He didn't flinch. Nothing in his expression twisted. It was as if he had no feeling there.

"Can you feel that?" I asked, worried that he'd somehow cut a nerve and no longer had feeling in his finger.

He let out his breath, pain contorting his face. "Yeah, I can feel that."

Whew. It would not go over well if I had to drag him into a hospital.

"Why were you acting like you couldn't?" I asked. I located the butterfly closures and slathered his cut with some antibacterial cream.

He shrugged. "I'm not the kind of person who likes to show weakness."

I eyed him, fighting the urge to roll my eyes. "You're one of those manly men?" I made sure that the butterfly closures were going to hold the skin together as I applied two next to each other.

"It must be interesting to see me through your eyes." He chuckled.

His response confused me as I wrapped gauze around his finger. "What?"

"Well, in a matter of twenty-four hours, you've called me sexy and a manly man." He shrugged.

I scoffed. "You think that I see you that way?" I ripped a piece of tape off with my teeth and secured the gauze. Then I leaned back and gave him my full attention.

"Well, don't you? I mean, you can't be speaking for

anyone else." He raised his hands and motioned toward the room. "There's no one else here."

My cheeks were warm. Sure, I thought he was attractive and manly, but I couldn't be the only one. Right?

I crumpled the bandage wrappers and began to put things back in the box. "Was there a reason you called me tonight? Besides wanting to make fun of me while I'm in a sleep-starved state." I sighed as I flipped my hair from my face and met his gaze head-on.

His smile faded, and he glanced down at the ground for a moment before he shrugged. "Besides Colten, you're the only other person I know in town." He sighed as he relaxed his back and glanced around the room. "And Colten didn't answer."

Great. I was second on the list of two people Jackson knew. "You know, you could solve this friend problem by going out. The town won't bite, and I've been here long enough to know that you aren't a vampire." I bumped his shoulder as I walked by him.

Tingles erupted across my skin at the point of contact. It startled me. I wanted to reach up and rub the feeling away, but I was carrying the first aid kit. So I was stuck allowing it to expand across my skin and throughout my body.

By the time I got back downstairs after putting the kit away, Jackson was up and standing in front of one of the far windows. He had the blinds cracked slightly and was staring outside. I scoffed as I descended the last step.

"So it's okay if you open the blinds but not me?" I

asked as I approached him. I folded my arms and studied him.

He glanced over his shoulder and paused before he stepped back, allowing the blind to fall against the window. It banged a few times as it settled in place. "It's not the opening of the blinds that I don't like," he said as he folded his arms to mirror my stance. He leaned one shoulder against the window divider and, a moment later, met my gaze.

He held it there for a moment, and like an idiot, I allowed him to. There was something in his eyes. An ache that I'd never seen before. Something was going on with him, but he was keeping it a secret.

I knew it was unrealistic to expect that he would answer my questions, but I wanted to know what he was thinking. I wanted to know what he was going through. I wanted to help in any way I could, and it was a desire that was growing stronger every time I was near him.

What was he hiding?

"Thanks." The depth of his voice as it broke the silence sent shivers down my spine. He could go from joking to serious in a matter of moments. It was disconcerting.

Not sure how to respond, I just offered him a smile. "Sure. I'm happy to help." Then I dropped my arms and motioned toward his finger. "Although if you get a cut that goes any deeper, you'll want to call the ambulance." I laced my fingers together and stretched them out in front of me. I tipped my head from one side to the other. "I'm good, but I'm not *reattach-your-finger* kind of good."

He glanced down at his hand, flexing his finger as far as the bandage would let him and then glanced back up at me. "I'll keep that in mind."

I nodded. "And maybe don't try to cut an apple in the middle of the night?"

He straightened his stance and gave me a salute. "Yes, ma'am."

I shook my head at him but allowed the smile on my lips to widen.

"I should go—"

"Do you want some coffee—"

We both stopped as we stared at the other.

"You can go—"

"Coffee might be good—"

We both pinched our lips. I raised my eyebrows and Jackson nodded.

"I'll get the coffee started."

I put the chairs back by the table while Jackson got the coffee brewing. When it was finished, we were both sitting at the table with a steaming mug in front of us. I fiddled with my mug's handle as I waited for it to cool.

Jackson was bouncing his knee and shifting in his seat.

Was he nervous to be around me?

I peeked over at him, trying to read his body language. What did he have to be nervous about? Maybe he just wanted me to drink my coffee and then get out of there.

His nervous energy was racing through me, so I picked up my coffee and took a big swig.

Bad idea.

The heat touched my lips and burned my tongue in an instant. Without thinking, I spat the coffee everywhere. My eyes were watering as I fanned my mouth. Anything to cool it down.

"Are you okay?" Jackson asked. He was up out of his chair.

"My mouth," I whispered as pain seared through my whole head.

Jackson disappeared, and a moment later, I heard the freezer door open. He returned with a glass of ice water. He handed it to me, and I gingerly took a sip. I continued to try to cool my mouth down while Jackson did something in the kitchen—I wasn't sure what he was up to, but I really didn't care.

My mouth hurt.

A few minutes later, Jackson returned with a heaping bowl of ice cream. "This'll help."

I nodded as I gingerly took a bite. It not only soothed my aching mouth, but also appeased my growling stomach. When the bowl was half-empty, I slowed, sitting back to find Jackson studying me.

He looked as if he were holding back a question, and I wasn't sure if I was prepared to find out what he wanted to say.

Finally—when I felt certain I was going to melt under his scrutiny—I asked, "What?"

He leaned back, his focus not changing. "Why did you try to down that coffee?"

I picked up my spoon once more and pushed the ice cream around in the bowl. Then I shrugged. "I thought you wanted me to get going."

"What made you think that?"

"You were acting all agitated."

"I was?"

I nodded and used the spoon to point to his knee. "You were bouncing your knee and shifting around like me being here was bugging you."

He dropped his gaze down to his leg. Then he sighed and shook his head. "If I didn't want you here, I wouldn't have hired you, and I certainly wouldn't have called you in the middle of the night." He pushed his hair from his face, and for the second time since I'd met him, I got a look at the scar that ran down his cheek.

It was only a glimpse before the hair fell back into place. I wondered what that meant. He wasn't hiding it; he'd knowingly moved his hair and exposed it.

Was he…trusting me?

A strange sense of excitement rushed through me at the thought. The fact that he didn't go anywhere and didn't allow others into his house made his invitations to me mean that much more. At the same time, it made me question, why me?

"Oh," I said softly. I wasn't sure how I was supposed

to respond, and from the uncomfortable look on Jackson's face, he looked unsure as well.

We sat in silence until my ice cream was gone. Then I stood and moved to grab my bowl at the same time Jackson did. Our fingers brushed each other, which sent my heart racing. I swallowed as I glanced up to see him staring hard at our hands.

Did he feel something too?

That was stupid. Don't ask yourself that.

That question was never going to end well.

Not wanting to linger any longer, I pulled my hands away and stepped back. I cleared my throat as I glanced around. "I should go. I need to get some sleep, or I'm going to be a bear for Blake. He's an early riser."

Jackson straightened with the bowl in his hands and nodded. "Okay."

I made my way to the door, and he followed after me, slipping the dishes into the sink as he passed by. After my shoes were on, I grabbed my purse and pulled my keys from the pocket.

Jackson leaned forward to open the door. That movement brought him closer to me, and his chest brushed against my shoulder. I startled from his closeness, taking a step back just to put space between us.

Whatever was happening scared me. Whether it was coming from me or him, I needed to put a stop to it. He wasn't anyone I could even be remotely interested in. I needed to make sure he knew he shouldn't be remotely interested in me.

The last thing I needed was to complicate my life with another relationship that could end up where all my relationships seemed to go—the crapper. I couldn't hold onto anything good, and right now, the good I was getting from Jackson was a paycheck.

There was no way I was going to compromise that.

"Thanks," Jackson said as he held the door for me.

I stepped out onto the deck and then turned, giving him a friendly smile. "That's what friends are for." I held onto my purse strap as I tried to interpret his gaze.

If he was bothered by my labeling of our relationship, he didn't show it. Instead he nodded and gave me another salute.

"See you tomorrow?"

I smiled. "See you tomorrow."

NINE

Penny

I decided the next morning when I woke up that I was going to visit Jackson. He was the reason I'd come to Magnolia, and even though I was enjoying my time here, I needed to focus on my end goal —keeping my job.

I showered and dressed in an outfit that looked dressy casual. Even though I'd spent most of my time here in jeans and flats, I needed to show Jackson that I meant business. Magnolia ran at a different speed than New York, and it was easy to slip into the relaxed atmosphere.

I was in the dining room, smearing cream cheese on a bagel when Maggie stepped up to me.

"You look nice," she said.

I glanced over and smiled. "I've got some work to do." I took a bite of my bagel, chewed, and swallowed before I continued. "I should be back by the afternoon." I wanted to make sure that she knew I was willing to help, but I also didn't want her to feel like she needed to include me if she didn't want to. "So if you want me for anything, I'll be around then."

Maggie lifted the top of the chafing dish to check the status of the French toast before she responded. "I think we are meeting with the florist at three." She glanced over her shoulder. "It would be fun if you could come."

Determined to make more of an effort, I nodded. "That should work." I offered her a smile. "Text me the address."

Maggie moved down the table to check another chafing dish while she mumbled her agreement. With my afternoon booked, I left the inn and headed to my rental car.

It didn't take long before I parked in Jackson's driveway and made my way around the house to the front door. It was eight in the morning. I figured he'd be in bed, but I didn't care. I'd given him space and time, and he needed to come back now.

Not only for me, but for himself and his fans.

Naomi had been skeptical that I'd be able to convince Jackson to return. She said once he got a thought in his mind, there was no changing it. However, I was confident that I could be just as stubborn as he was. He was about to meet his match.

I knocked a few times, and to my surprise, the door swung open seconds later. Jackson must have been expecting someone else, because as soon as his gaze fell on me, his smile disappeared.

"Oh," he said as he moved to shut the door.

I was faster than him and stepped forward right into the opening. When he realized that I wasn't going anywhere, he moved away from the door and let me in.

I shut the door and slipped off my shoes. "Were you expecting someone else?"

He plopped down on the couch with his legs extended and his head resting on the back. His eyes were closed, and I tried not to sigh when I realized that I was most likely not going to get anywhere with this man today. It was like I was dealing with an obstinate teenager.

And it grated on my nerves.

I moved to the living room and sat down on the armchair perpendicular to the couch. I crossed my legs, resting my hand on my lap as I studied him. What was going on that had him acting like this? I narrowed my eyes. There was nothing I could think of that would have had this millionaire author running for the hills.

It was so strange.

Having enough of staring at him in the hope that the answer to my questions would just appear on his skin, I glanced around the house. "It looks nice in here. Have you been cleaning?"

Jackson just grunted. He didn't move, and his eyes remained closed.

He was quite the conversationalist.

I turned my attention back to him. Apparently, small talk was out of the picture. He wasn't having it, so I wasn't going to waste my breath. "Listen, Jackson, you have to realize that if we don't publish your book, you will have to pay back your advance *plus* interest."

I let those words linger in the air, hoping that he would feel the weight of them. He was one of our only authors that brought in seven figure advances. If he was going to pay that back, it would be a hefty sum.

"I'm fine with that," he said. But the tone of his voice had changed. I could tell that he wasn't happy.

Good. That was something I could work with.

"Fine? You're willing to throw away hundreds of thousands of dollars?"

He stilled before he opened one eye and peered over at me. A moment later he closed his eyes again. "Yes."

And just like that, the window I'd found slammed shut. I sighed and settled against the back of the chair. "You're making a mistake. You have your whole life in front of you. Why would you throw it away? Over what?"

I glanced over at him, hoping that he'd answer my question...but he didn't. He remained still as if my words weren't affecting him at all. I groaned and rubbed my temples. This was never going to work.

We were interrupted by three soft knocks on the front door. Jackson was off the couch and across the room with a speed that I didn't think him capable of. Either he was excited to see whoever was standing on the other side— or he was just ready to talk to someone other than me.

Knowing Jackson, it was the latter.

He swung the door open, and unlike his reaction to seeing me, his shoulders remained up and his demeanor was cheery. Fiona stood on the other side with a smile on her lips. She looked happy to be there, which was strange. Jackson was not a cheery person. If anything, his prickly personality scared off more people than it charmed.

This was an interaction I was intrigued to watch.

"You're late," Jackson barked, but he didn't slam the door. Instead, he let her in.

"Yes, I'm so sorry. Blake's fever was back, so I was scrambling to get him a different place to go." She blew out her breath, which tossed the strands of hair that had fallen in front of her face. It didn't take her long to spot me, and her brow furrowed. "Penny?" She glanced between Jackson and me. "What are you doing here?"

I stood and smoothed down the front of my pants. Before I could explain my connection to Jackson, he stepped forward.

"She's my investment manager and came by to give me an update on one of my investments." He glanced over his shoulder. "Right?"

Confused, I studied him. I contemplated telling Fiona that he was joking, but I saw the desperation in his gaze. Whatever was going on, he was determined to keep who he was from this woman. It was strange, but I wasn't here to judge. I was here to get him back to New York.

So I gave Fiona a smile and nodded. "That's right. It's one of the main reasons I came down here. That and seeing Maggie." I turned to Jackson, so he'd understand what I said next. If he wanted me to play this game, I was going to get something out of it. "He was on the verge of agreeing to a new investment, and now that I'm willing to do the work, he's willing to hear me out."

He raised his eyebrows at me, but as Fiona's gaze swept between us, his expression morphed into one of acceptance. "I'm willing to consider it."

Fiona must have sensed that there was more going on than we were letting on, because a moment later, she shrugged and made her way into the kitchen. "Well, don't mind me. I'm just here to cook and clean." She pulled open the fridge door.

"Cook and clean?" I asked, turning my attention back to Jackson.

Before he could answer, Fiona responded. "He's hired me as his housekeeper." She gave me a smile that was a mixture of gratitude and relief. "It's really a lifesaver for me."

That was strange. For as long as I'd worked with Jackson, I'd never known him to let people into his life willy-nilly. He was guarded. What was it about Fiona that had him letting her in?

Apparently, Jackson didn't want me to find out. Before I knew what was happening, he ushered me to the front door. "Thanks for stopping by," he said.

I stared at him. Why was he acting this way? "We're not done with our conversation."

His hand found my elbow. He squeezed it as he studied me. "We can talk about this later."

I quirked an eyebrow. Was he serious?

He must have sensed my hesitation. He sighed and nodded. "I'll call you tomorrow."

Relived that I wasn't going to leave with no progress made, I nodded. "Deal," I said as I extended my hand.

Jackson looked down and then back up at me. I held his gaze, so he knew that I was serious. He looked annoyed, but he reached out and grabbed my hand, giving it a shake. I knew Jackson. His handshake was his word, and I was going to make sure that he knew I meant business.

"Deal," he muttered under his breath. Then he pulled open the door and waved me out.

Feeling a little closer to my goal, I headed out onto the porch. Fiona called a goodbye to me, but before I could answer, Jackson shut the door. Now alone, I turned my attention to the ocean.

I felt...lighter.

Maybe it was because of the fresh air washing over me. Or the sun rising in the sky, warming me with its rays. Maybe it was because I was spending time with my daughter and attempting to mend the fence that I'd destroyed.

But I think the biggest reason was that I was getting further along in my goal to win over Jackson. I was finding a way to crack him, and it felt...amazing.

I'd felt so down in New York. My whole life had been

crashing down around me. But here, I felt in control. I was in charge of my own destiny. I could get where I wanted to go.

I glanced down at my watch. I had a few hours before I needed to meet Maggie at the florist. I'd gotten as far as I could with Jackson today, so I might as well take my time and explore Magnolia. I enjoyed my time with Clementine yesterday. Walking through places that I used to frequent had brought out a sort of nostalgia inside of me.

Experiencing more of the town felt like the perfect way to spend my afternoon.

After all, I wanted to improve myself while I was here. Might as well start with facing my past.

I soon found myself pulling over on Main Street and parking my rental alongside Engrins, the local grocery store. My eyes roamed over the building. I marveled at how different it looked, and at the same time, how much it hadn't changed. It was strange. The bones were still there, but the decorations were different.

In a way, I felt like it represented me. I may look different. I may be older, but I was still the same inside. Funny how life is like that sometimes.

I waited for a red truck to pass before I pulled open my door and got out. After I shouldered my purse, I crossed the street. The smell of flowers wafted around me, causing me to breathe in deeply. Magnolia certainly knew how to create an atmosphere that made a person want to stay forever.

I wandered down the sidewalk, peering into the assorted shops. They had changed since I was here last. I waved at Jake when I passed by the hardware store, and he responded with an enthusiastic head nod. Just as I neared the corner, a shot of nostalgia rushed over me when I saw *Magnolia Daily*. The same blue sign sat above the small brick building. A place I knew like the back of my hand.

My foray into writing started as a reporter for the local newspaper. It was both thrilling and saddening to see the place. It had been my life when I lived here. So many parts of my past were showcased between its pages.

My wedding. My father's death. Even the birth of Maggie. In a small town, people loved to hear the happenings of the residents.

The newspaper was simple, but people loved it.

I loved it.

Without hesitation, I crossed the street and stood in front of the darkened glass door. One tug and the door swung open. The familiar scents of stress and paper wafted around me as I stepped inside.

"Yes, I know, Mrs. Tristie, but that's not something I do."

I peered around the corner to find a young woman sitting with her feet propped up on a desk and a phone cradled between her cheek and shoulder.

"I know *you* think it's newsworthy, but people don't want to read about how your cocker spaniel gave birth to seven puppies."

She paused before sighing.

"I'm sorry, award-winning cocker spaniel."

I chuckled. Different time, same conversation. I remembered sitting at a desk, fielding submissions just like this.

"Yes, I know you've been a lifelong subscriber...I know you've had this printed before, Mrs. Tristie. Mrs. Tristie..."

She was losing this fight. Taking pity on her, I decided to interrupt. "Excuse me?"

The girl whipped around, her eyes wide. When she saw me, I raised my hand—the universal sign for *I come in peace*—and gave her a wide smile.

"I'll have to let you go, Mrs. Tristie. Someone is here." She paused as her gaze wandered around the room. "I'll talk to Georgette to see what she says. Yes. Okay, goodbye."

She hung up the phone and then turned to me. "Sorry about that. Small town." She rested her elbow on her desk as she leaned toward me. "What can I help you with? Are you visiting? I've never seen you before."

I shrugged as I moved to run my fingers across the small shelf on the far wall. It held all the awards that our little newspaper had collected. "You could say that I'm a visitor of sorts. It's been a while since I've been back." I turned and gave her a smile.

She raised her eyebrows. "Back? So you lived here once?"

I nodded. "A long time ago."

"I'm back," The front door opened, and Georgette appeared. My entire body froze as I was face-to-face with my old editor and friend. She had pure white hair and wrinkles, but she looked just like I remembered her.

When her gaze locked with mind, she stopped and stared. Then a smile played on her lips as she set the white takeout bag and drink carrier she was holding onto the table at the entrance.

"As I live and breathe," she said as she threw her arms around me. "Lucky Penny has returned home."

I laughed out loud at the nickname she'd given me. "What are you still doing here?" I asked as I pulled away. She was ten years older than me, which meant she was four years from seventy.

Georgette pulled back. Her eyebrows were lifted, and her lips were pursed. "You know this place would fall apart without me. Plus, this place is like my husband. I can't just walk away from him."

"You walked away from two husbands," I said as I leaned in.

"Three, and yes, it's because they were jealous. No one wants to share Georgette."

I chuckled. "Man, some things never change."

Georgette patted my hand. "I would say the same to you." Then she motioned toward the woman at the desk. "I see you met my granddaughter, Lucy."

Lucy stood and extended her hand.

"Penny," I said. Then I shrugged. "Or Lucky Penny if you prefer."

"Penny is good. It's nice to meet you."

"Likewise." We shook, and when we pulled apart, Georgette stepped between us. She stuck her hand out in the direction of her office. "We have lots to catch up on."

I nodded. "We really do."

"Lucy, your taco is in the bag. I'm taking my lunch with Penny."

Lucy was already making her way to the food bag. She pulled out a white Styrofoam container. "Got it." Then she paused. "Hold your calls?"

Georgette glanced at me and then nodded. "Yep."

TEN

Fiona

---

*J*ackson was quieter today, which meant silence engulfed the house, as he wasn't that much of a chatterbox to begin with. Besides the occasional tease, he was a closed book. I knew nothing about him. When I tried to pry, I just discovered that there were more layers to him than I'd originally anticipated.

I wanted to know more, but I doubted that revealing those secrets was high on his list of priorities.

So I was stuck wiping down counters until my face showed in the dark granite as I wondered why he had called me last night.

Me.

Not his friend, the sheriff. Not his family. Not even the paramedics.

Me.

Was that normal? I glanced over at my phone and

contemplated searching *normal duties of a housekeeper* but then pushed that thought from my mind. I didn't need an internet search to know the answer.

It was strange. I had no idea what it meant.

Jackson shifted on the couch as he leaned forward and grabbed some grapes from the bowl on the coffee table. He was watching some sport—I didn't bother to investigate which, as sports really weren't my thing—and his gaze was affixed to the screen. Every so often, he'd shout, and I couldn't quite tell if his bellow was one of joy or frustration.

I tapped my fingers on the countertop I'd just wiped as I studied him. I was beginning to realize that I knew nothing about this man. It was just another thing for me to file away in the things-I-don't-really-know-about-Jackson section of my brain.

That section was becoming crowded.

"Mind grabbing me a soda?"

Jackson's voice drifted into my thoughts, and it took me a moment to register that he'd said something. I blinked as I glanced over in his direction.

"Mmm?"

He raised his eyebrows. "A soda. From the fridge. Mind grabbing me one?"

As if on autopilot, probably because I was constantly fulfilling Blake's wishes, I moved to the fridge and pulled open the door. After a quick scan, I grabbed a can of root beer.

Jackson watched me as I crossed the room. There was

this intensity to his gaze that made my entire body flush. It was as if he were studying my every move. Was that possible? Or was I just reading into things because I wanted to be seen?

Working. Being a mom. Living above the coffee shop. I was quickly losing who I was as a woman. It was getting to the point where I was forgetting who Fiona was and what I liked.

"You okay?"

I startled and glanced down only to realize that I was standing in front of Jackson, holding out the soda. He had grabbed the bottom of the can, but since I hadn't released it, we were in a stalemate. His brow was furrowed as he studied me.

Exhaustion took over. I let go and collapsed on the couch next to him. I tried to ignore his confused look as I sat there with one arm draped over my forehead like some actress from the fifties.

I was tired, and part of my exhaustion came from him waking me up in the middle of the night to come repair his finger. I shifted my elbow, so I could look at his hand without him knowing that I was looking. The bandage was still there. I felt a sense of pride that I'd done such a good job. I guess when your patient isn't a wriggly toddler, it's easier to affix a bandage without accidentally folding the tabs in on themselves and sticking them together.

"I'm tired," I whispered, finally answering his question.

"Ah." He made a fist with his bandaged hand as if he knew what I was referring to. Which was nice. It meant that he wasn't oblivious to the fact that he'd asked a lot of me last night.

I dropped my arm and blew out my breath. "Not just that. Blake's been so crabby. I can't tell if he's getting his molars or if he's sensing my stress, and it's rubbing off on him."

When Jackson didn't respond right away, I peeked over at him. He was studying the soda in front of him. He hadn't popped the tab yet and was fiddling with the edges of the can. His frown accented his dimples on either side of his mouth.

How had I not seen his dimples before?

The silence between us ticked on, which only made me feel even more like an idiot. I chastised myself for sharing so much. I doubted that he wanted to know my life story, and here I was, oversharing. As always.

"Sorry," I whispered as I moved to stand.

His gaze snapped up to meet mine, freezing me in place. "Where are you going?" he asked.

I furrowed my brow. "I was going to go back to cleaning your kitchen. Why? Did you want me to stick around?"

He shrugged. "I just thought we were talking."

"Really?"

He nodded.

Relief flooded my body. I wasn't ready to get up just yet. My muscles screamed as I tried to move them, so I'd take any excuse to stay seated. Plus, I was going to just sidestep the fact that he said we were "talking." Our conversation so far had been pretty one-sided, with me talking and him listening—but I wasn't going to point that out.

If he was willing to pay me to sit and stare at him, who was I to complain?

"How's your hand?" I asked, motioning toward his bandage.

"I'll survive."

"Is it going to impede your work as a..." I narrowed my eyes. "A comic book artist?"

His frown deepened. "A what?"

I laughed, sitting up straighter and bringing my feet up to rest under me. "I'm trying to figure out what you do."

"And comic book artist is the best you've come up with?"

I raised my hands. "Hey, you have to start somewhere." I wrapped my arms around my legs as I held them to my chest. "So no on the comic book artist."

He shook his head. "I can't even draw a stick figure well."

I laughed wholeheartedly, and it felt great. It had been so long since I'd laughed like this that I'd forgotten how it made me feel.

Jackson was studying me when I finally composed myself. Realizing that I must have looked crazy, laughing like that, I cleared my throat and shrugged. "Sorry."

"Comedian isn't my profession either, but from your reaction, I'm starting to wonder if it should be."

I rolled my eyes. "If your ideal audience is exhausted single mothers, then you'll be a hit." I reached out and playfully swatted his arm. What started out as a reflex quickly became a mistake as my fingers brushed his skin. The warmth radiated across my hand and into my chest as my heart began to pound.

What was wrong with me? Why was I touching him?

"Sorry," I mumbled as I moved to stand. "I should get back to work."

I wanted to pretend that Jackson wasn't as startled by my touch as I was, but that would be a lie. His lips were pursed, and he looked as if he'd swallowed a lemon as I hurried back across the room. What had started out as a normal, healthy conversation had quickly turned into a mess in a matter of moments.

Honestly, I should have known that would happen. After all, my life was a series of mistakes. I never could make the right decision. Interacting with Jackson wasn't an exception.

I blew out my breath as I turned my back to Jackson and started cleaning the oven. I'd spent most of my time here cleaning the kitchen, so it didn't take long before the surfaces were sparkling. Jackson didn't seem to do very much in this room, and I'd been so diligent that there was very little to wipe away.

I found myself finishing the room in under half an hour.

Not sure what to do, I moved to sweeping the dining room. Jackson had finally opened the soda I'd given him and settled back on the couch. He wasn't as animated as he resumed watching the game. Instead, he just sat there as if there were something weighing on his mind.

Which I hoped had nothing to do with me.

The shrill sound of my phone ringing startled me. I quickly reached into my pocket and pulled it out. Bonnie, the last minute daycare lady, flashed across the screen.

Dread filled my chest as I pressed talk. "Hello?" I asked once I brought the phone to my cheek.

"Fiona?"

"Yeah."

"It's Blake. I think his fever spiked again. He's really crabby, and I'm worried he'll spread what he has to the other kids. Can you come get him?"

I could tell that Jackson was studying me from the corner of his eye. Not wanting him to worry, I turned so my back was to him. "Um, yeah. Let me call my mom to see if she can come get him."

"Okay, thanks. I want to help you out, but I can't if he could infect the other kids."

I nodded even though tears stung my eyes. I was too tired to fight back, and I knew if the roles were reversed, I'd want someone to keep their kid out of daycare so as to not infect Blake.

I called Mom, but after a quick conversation with her, I realized she wasn't going to be able to help. With me taking this job, she was left to man the coffee shop by herself. There was no way she was going to be able to do it all and watch Blake.

I was on my own.

I told Mom that I understood and hung up the phone. After slipping it back into my pocket, I closed my eyes and allowed a wave of self-pity to wash over me. I was frustrated that I was going to have to end my day here early. I was frustrated that Dave wasn't here to help me out.

I was frustrated that Blake was sick.

But most of all, I was frustrated that I was frustrated.

This was my son. I should be there for him. Instead, I was racking my brain for ways I could get him picked up without leaving work. Even though I knew that was impossible, I wanted to exhaust all of my options before I gave up.

Did that make me a bad mom?

"Everything okay?" Jackson called to me. He'd tipped his head in my direction with his gaze still fixed on the screen.

I took a moment to compose myself before I turned around and offered him a wide smile. "Yeah, sorry. That was Blake's daycare. His fever is back, so I'm going to have to cut today short, if you don't mind."

Jackson's gaze drifted over to me. He studied me for a moment before he said, "Yeah, I kind of do mind."

At first, I thought I'd misheard him. I furrowed my brow as I stared at him. But the longer I held his gaze, the more I began to realize I'd heard him right. He didn't want me to leave.

"I have to get him. There's no one else who can watch him."

Jackson shrugged as he picked up the remote and began to flip through the channels. "I need my bathroom cleaned today."

Heat pricked at the back of my neck. Was he serious? He wanted me to put off picking up my son because he needed me to clean his bathroom? I understood that he was paying me to clean his house. But he had to understand that I needed to leave. I had no choice.

"Well, apart from bringing Blake here, there's nothing else I can do. I have to leave." My hands found their way to my hips, and I rested them there. I needed to seem bigger and stronger than I was. My confidence was waning, that was for sure.

Jackson took his time flipping through the channels on the TV before he shrugged and said, "Then bring him here."

I blinked. "You want me to bring him here?" I asked, pointing at the floor to make sure he understood what he was saying.

"Yeah. Bring him here. We can hang out, and you don't have to lose a day of work."

Tears gathered behind my eyelids. Was he being nice or was he trying to control me? He didn't look demanding. If anything, he looked apathetic. Did he really want me to stay, or was this just a ploy?

Feeling completely confused, I cleared my throat and straightened. "If you're okay with my son hanging out here, then I'll bring him. Heaven knows I need the money." I winced at my declaration.

The last thing I needed was for this stranger to know just how bad things were for me financially. Besides the book club, no one else on the island knew what was happening to Mom and me. The bank had come back and given us an ultimatum. We had until the end of next month to come up with half the money she owed, or they were going to foreclose on the property.

With money from the coffee shop and my earnings here, we were on the cusp of hitting that number. So if Jackson was going to help me stay on track, I was going to take him up on that offer. But that didn't mean I needed to unload my dirt on him.

I didn't want him to know just how desperate I was. But if I kept talking like that, he was going to catch on.

Jackson nodded in recognition and then turned his attention back to the TV. I grabbed my phone and texted Bonnie to let her know I was coming. She responded with a thumbs-up. I threw on my shoes and hurried from the house.

Blake was tired when I picked him up. He whimpered a bit and rested his head on my shoulder as I carried him from daycare. Bonnie kept apologizing, but I told her it was okay. Blake wasn't feeling well, and he should stick with me if that was the case.

After I buckled him in, I contemplated taking him

straight home and calling Jackson to tell him I wasn't going to come. But I pushed that from my mind. After all, if Blake was just going to sleep at the apartment, then he could sleep at Jackson's while I worked.

Mom guilt was real, and I was discovering that it was hard to be the provider as well as the nurturer. Blake needed a mom to snuggle with, but he also needed someone to fund his needs. Without help from Dave, I had to be both even if they conflicted with each other.

Blake was asleep when I pulled into Jackson's driveway. I turned off the engine, and just as I moved to get out, movement caught my eye. I focused on the man standing at the edge of the porch only to realize that it was Jackson.

What was he doing out here?

I slipped my keys into my purse and got out. Jackson must have realized it was me and hurried over. I ran my gaze over him, wondering if he'd injured himself, but he seemed fine.

"Hey," I said, not sure how else I was supposed to address the fact that he was standing right next to my car, peering into the back window.

"I thought you might need help bringing Blake in."

I shouldered my purse as I studied him and then glanced in at Blake. "You want to help me bring in Blake?"

Jackson's expression was strained for a moment before he nodded. "Yeah."

That was it. One word to explain why he was

standing next to me, ready to help me with my son like his father should be doing.

I wasn't sure what to say, so I didn't say anything. I opened the door and unbuckled Blake. When I stepped back, Jackson dipped into the car and hoisted him up.

I walked quietly behind Jackson as we made our way to the front door. My gaze kept drifting to my son's peaceful face as he rested his head on Jackson's shoulder. I couldn't help but think that this was how a family should be. How much Blake was missing out because he didn't have a dad in his life.

How much I needed someone else's support in parenting my child.

It really took a village to raise a child, and that fact felt even more acute when you were lacking that village.

When we got into the house, Jackson brought Blake over to the couch where he'd set up a pillow and blanket. Blake whimpered when Jackson laid him down, so I took over, tucking him in and pushing his floppy brown hair from his face. It didn't take long before Blake settled down in the fluffy blanket and pillow.

I glanced over at Jackson, who had the TV remote in his hand and was turning the volume down. I had so many questions for him, but I didn't know where to start.

Why was he being so nice to me? Why was he being so nice to Blake?

Did he want something from me?

My heart had been broken enough in the past for me to know that everyone always wanted something.

If Jackson noticed my stare, he didn't say anything. Instead, he set the remote down on the table and moved to the kitchen. "I'm going to make some food," he said quietly.

Not wanting him to walk away before I could say anything, I followed.

"Thanks," I whispered.

Jackson stopped moving and slowly turned around to face me. His expression looked strained. "I grew up with a single mom. I saw how hard it is." His tone sounded strained as he pushed his hand through his hair.

My heart hurt for him. Whatever had happened in his past had affected him. And I wanted to know more. Jackson was a mystery that I was desperate to uncover.

I just wasn't sure if he felt the same.

I wasn't sure how to find out.

ELEVEN

Penny

I felt a profound familiarity as I sat in Georgette's office, watching her adjust her readers on the tip of her nose. We'd spent many afternoons here brainstorming articles and ideas back when I worked here. It was during those meetings that I fell in love with the written word.

Being able to craft a story in a way that inspired or enraged was a thrill. With the flick of my pen, I felt as if I could change the world.

The sound of a Styrofoam container drew my attention over to Georgette. She had a plastic fork and knife and was digging into what smelled like fajitas.

My stomach growled at the scent. I hadn't eaten lunch, and my bagel this morning had only lasted about an hour. Regardless, I didn't want to get up. This was the first time since I got here that I felt at home, and there was no way I was leaving now.

"So what are you doing back in Magnolia?" Georgette asked after a few bites of her food.

I wasn't sure how much I should tell her about Jackson—especially since I didn't know how to say it without making me sound like a complete failure. I decided to just shrug and say, "Maggie's getting married."

"I heard." She took a deep breath as she sat there with her elbows propped up on the armrests of her chair and her utensils sticking straight up in the air.

It was such a contrast to the uppity people I lunched with on the regular in New York. Here, things were simpler, and people were less judgmental. As much as I wanted to say that I'd outgrown this place, the truth was, I missed it.

"I'm here to help her plan."

Georgette nodded. "How's that going? She doesn't seem like a girl who stresses a whole lot."

I leaned forward. "You have that girl pegged. I swear, if I wasn't here, she and Archer would head to the justice of the peace and just get it over with." I sighed as I leaned back in my chair. "But I think it's good that she's making an effort. After all, her first marriage wasn't good. I like Archer, and I want this to last."

Georgette chewed as she studied me. Every so often, she nodded in agreement. "It's good that you came back. Dorthy always wanted you to return. It's a bummer that she never got to see that."

Talking about my mom made me uncomfortable, so I

shifted in my seat, hoping to change the subject before this got any deeper. "I'm happy to be back." Then I glanced around the room. "And happier to see that this place is still standing."

"You haven't thought about us since you left, have you?" Georgette wiped her lips with a paper napkin, removing half her red lipstick in the process. "I bet as soon as you drove over the bridge, it flew from your memory."

She wasn't wrong. I'd been so busy ever since I left that there really hadn't been time to think of anything else but my career. If my own daughter didn't take up that much of my headspace, an old job certainly wasn't going to make the cut. But I didn't want to be rude, so I just gave her a soft smile. "It may have crossed my mind once or twice."

Georgette bounced a few times on her chair as she held my gaze. Then she leaned forward. "Are they keeping you busy in New York? You're an editor now, right?"

Lately, any mention of my job always seemed to cause a knot to form in my stomach. I wasn't really in the mood to discuss how close I was to losing my job, so I was going to try hard to evade this topic.

"Yep. But I miss the thrill of journalism." I glanced around once more, allowing the memories to wash over me. Even though I may not have thought about this place, this building and the people inside of it always had a special place in my heart.

"Wanna come back?"

My gaze snapped back to Georgette. She had a completely serious expression on her face. "What?" I asked.

She shrugged. "I'm too old to be here. I'm just toughing it out until Lucy figures out her life—which she doesn't seem to be in a hurry to do."

"I heard that." Lucy's voice carried in through the closed door.

"Then do something about it," Georgette shouted back. I couldn't help but smile, enjoying the obvious love she had for her granddaughter even if she wanted that granddaughter to light a fire under herself.

Georgette set down her utensils and leaned back. She rested her elbows once more on the armrests and pressed her fingertips together. "I'd love to leave this place to a person who loves it as much as I do." She narrowed her eyes. "Are you still that person?"

My body felt light. The thought of returning to Magnolia to work at the newspaper I grew up on...well, it got my heart pumping harder than it had in a long time. Excitement coursed through me with each beat. I wanted to say no. I wanted to say that I'd be leaving a healthy income and stature, but who was I kidding? My job was on the line, and no one was rushing to hire a fifty-something woman.

I was past my prime in the publishing world, and it was only a matter of time before Burt and Kyle fully committed to firing me.

Words of acceptance were on the tip of my tongue, but I couldn't find it in myself to say yes. After all, maybe I was premature in my fear about my future at Sampson and Scotts. I would be a fool to walk away from something so good on the pretense that they were going to fire me.

I was still employed. I should lean on that.

So I gave Georgette a small smile. "I'll have to think about it."

She focused back on her food, seeming appeased. "You do that. I'm convinced that after some heavy thought you'll agree." She shrugged. "This was always your home, and people have a tendency to come back to where they started."

She wasn't wrong. I was discovering just how satisfying it was to walk my old stomping ground. It was both nostalgic and saddening at the same time. I was constantly surprised at the number of places that had changed, but I was equally surprised at the number of places that stayed the same.

One of the benefits of living in a small town: people were less likely to change up their surroundings. I was beginning to realize I liked that trait. New York was constantly changing. Constantly shifting. It was exhausting.

"See, I told you," Georgette said as she raised her fork and pointed it at me.

I shifted on my seat, hating that she could see through me. She always seemed to know what I was thinking before I had time to sort it out myself. "I don't know what you are talking about," I said as I flicked my hair over my shoulder.

"Mark my words, you'll be back here in a month begging me to take you in. You're going to get back to that fancy job of yours in the big city and discover how unhappy you are there. Especially after you lived the life you remembered here."

"We'll see," I muttered, hating how right she was. I *was* going to miss Magnolia. More now than ever.

"Mark my words," she repeated.

We spent the rest of her lunch hour reminiscing about Magnolia and who was divorced and who had died. I was happy to hear that most were still around. The people I grew up with were still alive and kicking. It gave me hope.

I might still have the time I needed to start over.

At two thirty, my phone chimed. I pulled it from my purse and looked down. Maggie had texted me the address of the florist, Petal Pushers. From what I could remember, it was in the same spot as a previous florist, so I knew exactly where it was.

"I should go," I said as I shouldered my purse.

Georgette nodded. "Yeah. I've got to get back to work." She pushed her chair back and stood. "If I want to have something to leave Lucy, I've got to do what I can to keep this place afloat."

I nodded. The weight of her words wasn't lost on me. I knew she had to be stressed if she was coming to me for help. Georgette wasn't one to admit that she was in trouble, and when she did, it meant she'd lost hope. I was her last resort.

"We'll have to get dinner some night while I'm here," I said as I led the way out of her office. Lucy was sitting at her desk, playing solitaire. As soon as she heard us, she clicked out of the game and turned to give me a smile.

The source of Georgette's desperation was becoming more apparent.

"I would love that. Maybe you can stop by my house, and I'll cook you some food. Is lobster tail still your favorite?"

I gave Georgette a quick hug. "Only the way you make it."

She pulled back and then clapped her hands. "It's settled. We'll meet for dinner sometime next week. Maybe by then you'll be ready to make Magnolia your home once more."

I gave her a weak smile. "We'll see."

I said goodbye to Lucy and then headed back outside. The sun was high in the sky, so I slipped on my sunglasses and headed to my car. It only took five minutes to drive to the florist. It surprised me that I could still find my way around Magnolia. It was like riding a bicycle. You never forget your hometown.

Archer's truck was parked in the lot, so I pulled in next to it. I hurried across the gravel to the shop's glass front door. A small bell chimed as I entered. Maggie and Archer looked up at the sound of my entrance. So did the small blonde woman on the other side of the counter.

"Hello," she said as she took a step toward me.

"It's okay, Olivia. This is Penny, my mom."

I gave Olivia a smile and then hurried over to stand next to Maggie. "Sorry I'm late. I got caught up at the newspaper."

Maggie's eyebrows went up. "You were at *Magnolia Daily?*"

I nodded. "I used to work there."

"You used to work there?"

This was an interesting conversation. "It was my job all throughout high school and a little bit after."

Maggie stood there with a dumbfounded look on her face. It confused me. I swore I'd told her this before.

"I had no idea," she whispered. "Archer, did you know?"

Archer glanced in my direction. He shook his head as he moved to place his hand on the small of her back. "I didn't, but it doesn't have much to do with flowers, so maybe we should finish here, and then we can continue this conversation."

Maggie glanced at me a few more times before she turned her attention back to Olivia. I could still see her surprised expression as Olivia listed off the flowers for the boutonnieres, the bouquet, and the corsages. I appreciated Maggie's attempt at trying to include me. Every time a photo was presented, she made sure to angle it, so I could see.

I was happy for my daughter, I was, but this wasn't my scene. It also didn't help that I was completely distracted by what Georgette had asked me. The fact that she wanted me back was strange. The fact that a part of me wanted to say yes was even stranger.

I mean, I made a solid six figures a year. Turning away from a job I'd given my life to was stupid, right? What proof did I have that Burt and Kyle wanted me gone? For all I knew it was just conjecture.

Was I willing to walk away from a good-paying job for a job that once meant so much to me?

Georgette had hinted that the paper was in trouble. How long before it folded? Was she wanting me to invest?

"I would be stupid," I whispered before I even realized that I'd spoken.

When all three sets of eyes turned on me, my entire body flushed. I pinched my lips together and offered them a sympathetic smile. "I'm sorry," I said as I tapped my lips. "My mind is somewhere else today."

There was something strained in Maggie's gaze, but it only lasted a moment before it disappeared and was replaced with her normal cheerful smile. "It's okay. You've been busy."

A wave of guilt washed over me. My daughter wanted me to be present, and I really wanted to do that for her. After all, I'd come here and told her that I wanted to help plan her wedding. What kind of mother would I be if I didn't at least attempt to give it my all?

Instead, I'd allowed myself to be distracted by Jackson, or the paper, or the memories that seemed to haunt me here. I'd promised to give this week to my daughter, but I was doing anything but.

"No, no. It's not okay. I allowed myself to get distracted." I leaned toward the book they were looking at and saw a beautiful bouquet of lilies, roses, and baby's breath. I tapped my finger on the arrangement. "I'd go with this one." A strange feeling settled in my stomach as I turned to face Maggie. "It looks just like the one I had when I married your father."

Her eyes glistened, and for a moment, I wondered if those were tears. She smiled and cleared her throat as she turned to face Olivia. "I guess we'll go with this one," she said.

Olivia grabbed a nearby notepad and started writing down the order. I watched as Maggie smiled up at Archer. He told her that it was beautiful before he leaned down and brushed his lips against hers.

A warmth started in my gut and radiated throughout my whole body. It was a feeling I got when I watched one of my book babies go out into the world, when I saw fans lining up to get their signed copies. It was a sense of accomplishment at seeing the final product you'd worked so hard to create.

Maggie wasn't a book; she was my daughter. And for the first time in a long time, it felt that way. It wasn't something I was used to. After all, the women in my family didn't show emotion. They didn't open up and allow people in.

Vulnerable wasn't in the Addington vocabulary. So seeing the happiness in Maggie's eyes as she picked flowers that were similar to mine sparked something deeper inside of me. Something that I hadn't realized that I wanted.

Maybe it was just satisfaction that I'd finally been able to help with this wedding planning gig. Or maybe I was happy because we were that much closer to the wedding day.

Or maybe, and this was a big maybe...

I wanted something more.

TWELVE

Fiona

J was completely distracted as I worked on cleaning Jackson's bathroom. He'd been so adamant on it being cleaned that I expected it to look like a bomb had gone off inside. But it was practically perfect.

Besides a few water spots on the faucet and a bit of grime around the toilet, the bathroom was clean. It made me wonder why he'd wanted to hire a housekeeper. He wasn't a particularly dirty person.

Add that confusion to my worry about Blake, and I was a hot mess.

When I caught a glimpse of myself in the mirror, I audibly gasped. My hair had fallen out of its bun, and the combination of sweat and humidity had turned it into a mess of curly flyaways. I looked like a mad scientist.

I rinsed my hands quickly and took a moment to fix

my hair. I wasn't trying to be attractive for Jackson or anything—I just didn't want to look like a dead-tired mommy.

I wanted to feel alive.

With my hair done, I worked to finish the bathroom. Once the surfaces were sparkling, I gathered the cleaning supplies and turned off the light. I deposited the supplies in the hall closet and slipped past Jackson's bedroom. It was just as clean as it had been yesterday.

The bed was made—with the corners tucked in military style. It was almost as if he hadn't slept on it. Without thinking, I moved closer to the bed. When I got there, I reached down and brushed my fingertips across his comforter. The fabric was soft and smooth.

Did he sleep here or the couch? He seemed to spend the majority of his time on the couch. If that was the case, why didn't he sleep in his bed?

Why was he even here?

"What are you doing?"

Jackson's voice startled me. I gasped and turned, yanking my hand away from the bed. My brain reeled as I tried to think of an excuse. A reason why I was standing here, fondling his comforter.

"I was—I mean, I am—." I cleared my throat. "I finished cleaning the bathroom."

His gaze drifted from me, over to the bathroom door, and then back to me. "So what are you doing to my bed?"

I clasped the hand that had been touching the

comforter. Heat permeated my body as I melted under his scrutiny. "I was just..." How could I say this without making me sound like a psycho? Realizing there was no way to do that, I decided to go with the truth. "Your bed was made like this last night when I was here."

He furrowed his brow. "And?"

I blew out my breath. "And I was wondering if you even sleep here."

There, I said it. Ugh, when had I turned into this loser?

Jackson was quiet for a moment before his lips tipped up into a smile. It was both strange and unsettling. Was this the kind of smile that a killer had right before they murdered their victim?

"You've been picturing me sleeping?" His words were marked with a laugh. It was low and throaty and...sexy.

Even though I found myself getting distracted, I had to address what he'd said. There was no way I was going to let that slide.

"I wasn't doing that," I whispered. Great. All of my confidence erased by one simple question.

"Mm-hmm," Jackson said as he folded his arms and leaned against the railing behind him. "You're touching my bed. Wondering where I sleep." He narrowed his eyes as he circled his forefinger in my direction. "You can't stop thinking about me."

I glowered at him and planted my hands on my hips. "That is not what I said." I cleared my throat, suddenly finding my strength again. "I simply noticed that your bed looked perfect, and it made me wonder if you slept in it. That's all."

Jackson just kept his lips pursed as he nodded—his eyebrows raised the entire time. He was teasing me, and I wasn't sure what I thought about that. I didn't want to care what he thought…but I did.

I wanted him to stop thinking that I cared about him, like I was trying to pretend that I didn't.

Jackson pushed off the railing and took a few steps toward me. "I didn't mean to upset you," he said. His voice had dropped an octave. It went right from friendly banter to concern.

Feeling like a sensitive idiot, I shook my head. "You didn't upset me. I just want to make sure that our boundaries are established."

"Boundaries?" He frowned as he studied me.

I felt like I was digging a hole for myself, and instead of climbing out, I just kept making it worse. "Yeah. Between us," I said as I waved my hand between his chest and mine.

"What do you think will happen if we don't set these boundaries?" He stepped closer again. The playfulness in his voice returning.

The implication caused heat to rise to my cheeks once more. I wanted to think that we were just having a friendly conversation, as boss and employee, but I was starting to think that something else was going on. Was it possible that he saw me as something more?

I needed to speak if I was going to keep the upper

hand in this conversation. I parted my lips. "I don't know," I whispered.

Jackson took another step forward. He was a mere foot away from me now. He was staring down at me with the same intensity that he seemed to have every time he looked at me. It was as if he were trying to see every part of me.

"Really?" he asked, his voice deepening.

It sent shivers down my spine.

"Yeah."

He inched closer to me. He wasn't touching me, but I felt the heat of his body as he stood there, staring at me. I could feel the tension between us, and it made me wonder…could he?

His lips tipped up into a smile as he leaned in. "I—"

"Mommy?"

I snapped back, ripping my focus from Jackson's face as I glanced behind him. "Blake?" I asked, grateful for this break in concentration. I was fairly certain I'd been about to do something that I could never recover from. Though there was no walking back from the thoughts that were racing through my mind.

The familiar sound of a child vomiting had me quickening my pace. By the time I got down the stairs and over to Blake, the front of his shirt and the blanket in his lap were covered in throw-up. Breathing through my mouth, I picked him up—while trying to keep the rest of the mess in the blanket—and hurried him to the lower-level bathroom. Once inside, I stripped him out of his clothes and began to rinse him off.

I was completely embarrassed.

First, the whole scene that had played out upstairs had been...humiliating. I wasn't someone who flirted. Being covered in throw-up and snot had a humbling effect on a woman. To think I even attempted it only solidified in my mind that I was to never do that again.

Second, my son just vomited all over Jackson's couch. He was a single man who liked his solitude, and now his solitude involved the sour smell of whatever had been churning in Blake's tummy.

If he wasn't going to fire me because of my botched attempt at flirting, he was going to now. How does one even come back from this?

Blake seemed to feel better once I had him cleaned off. I got most of the vomit on his shirt into the toilet, and the rest I rinsed out in the sink. All the while, Blake sat in the corner with my phone, watching his favorite kid show. His cheeks were pink, but he was smiling as his favorite bear danced across the screen.

Whatever was bothering him seemed to have been appeased for now.

Blowing my hair from my face, I took a moment to sanitize Jackson's bathroom, wrap up Blake's clothes in a spare garbage bag, and wash my hands thoroughly.

After attempting to comb my hair back into a bun —with no success—I decided the best thing to do was to gather the vomit-soaked blanket, my son, and what was left of my dignity, and hightail it out of Jackson's house.

After giving myself a little pep talk, I pulled open the bathroom door. Blake followed behind me in his underwear, still clutching my phone in his hands. I glanced around to see where Jackson was—but was relieved to see that we were alone.

I hurried into the kitchen, where I grabbed a large garbage bag and shook it out. Then I headed into the living room and stopped.

The blanket—the one that Blake had thrown up on—was gone.

Worry washed over me as I followed the path I'd taken to the bathroom. Had I accidentally dragged it along with me? I could only imagine what it would take to get the vomit out of the couch.

But I didn't see it anywhere.

I turned in a circle, completely confused. Had it grown legs and wandered off?

Just as I made my second spin around the room, the front door opened. Jackson slipped into the room wearing sunglasses and a pair of rubber gloves. He startled when his gaze met mine.

Without saying a word, he pulled his gloves off and made his way into the kitchen to toss them into the garbage before washing his hands.

"Did you…" I shook my head. There was no way this strange man had helped take care of Blake's mess. Dave didn't even do that when we lived with him—and Blake was his child. "Have you seen the blanket that Blake" —I paused, humiliated that I was going to say these words to my employer— "threw up on?"

Jackson dried his hands. When he was finished, he turned to the oven and pulled it open to reveal a pizza that had been cooking. He moved it around on the stone before shutting the door. "I took care of it," he said as he turned back around, leaning against the counter as he studied me.

"You..." I scoffed. Was this a joke? "You took care of his throw-up?"

He winced at that word. "I'd prefer we don't talk about it, but yes. I just threw the blanket away."

My embarrassment only grew stronger. "I'm so sorry. I'll replace it as soon as I can."

Jackson raised his hand. "That's not necessary. The blanket came with the house. I'm not attached to it." He shrugged. "It was kind of ugly anyway."

"Oh." I stood there, feeling like an idiot. How do you thank your boss for cleaning up your son's vomit? Was there, like, a greeting card for that?

Jackson looked at ease as he stood there with his arms folded. He didn't look like the emotional wreck that I was. It had to be nice to be the person with all the power.

He had money. He was my boss. He was doing nice things for me that he wasn't getting paid for. Sure, I helped him out, but he wrote me a check. Could I really claim sainthood when helping him benefited me?

"You worry too much," Jackson said as he shifted his weight.

"I do?" I was tired. I was exhausted. And knowing my son, I had an evening of vomit-soaked clothes ahead of me. Worrying just came with the job description.

He nodded. "When was the last time you just had some time to yourself?"

I laughed. Loud. "Myself? Geez, I don't even know what that looks like."

He furrowed his brow. I could tell he didn't like my response. He looked...worried.

Not sure how to take that, I cleared my throat and shrugged. "I'd say the closest I get to a break is our local book club. We have a meeting coming up, and I'm ready for it." I sighed. "I need it."

"A book club?" There was something about those words that had him standing a little taller. His normally brooding expression had shifted to one of interest.

"Ah, a fellow bibliophile?" I asked, allowing my voice to slip into one of teasing. And then I instantly regretted it. What was I doing? Was I flirting *again*?

It had been so long since Dave and I had dated, and there was no way I was going to even attempt a romantic relationship with a child, so I wasn't even sure how to do it if I wanted to. What I was doing in this moment was not something I should ever do.

Especially not with the man who hired me.

I cleared my throat and shook my head. "I'm sorry. I don't know what that was." My cheeks were warm, and I wanted nothing more than for the ground to open up and swallow me whole.

"It's okay." Jackson shrugged and leaned in. "And yes, I loved reading."

My brows furrowed. "Loved? Past tense?"

An expression passed over Jackson's features, and I wasn't sure what it meant. He looked almost…sad. Like there was something in his past that he was keeping hidden.

What did it have to do with books?

Blake whimpered. He'd wandered over to the couch while Jackson and I were talking. His skin had paled, so I scooped him up and hurried to the bathroom. Thankfully, he didn't throw up until I got him to the toilet. The volume was less than the first episode, which had me hoping that his stomach would settle soon.

I washed him up and brought him back out to the couch, where I found a new blanket had appeared. The fabric was worn; parts of the applique were fraying. It looked sentimental—nothing like the previous blanket that Blake had thrown up on.

I glanced over my shoulder, wondering if Jackson had placed it here for me to use. If it did mean something to him, I really didn't want to use it for my sick child. I almost died when Jackson said he threw the previous blanket away. If Blake got sick on this one and it met the same fate, I would never live it down.

"You can use it." Jackson's voice carried from the kitchen.

I startled and glanced over my shoulder to see him straighten up from behind the counter. He had an oven mitt and was lifting the pizza stone with a steaming hot pizza out of the oven. It smelled amazing, and it made me realize that I was starving. Besides the plain toast I had this morning on my way out the door, I hadn't eaten anything else.

With the whole Blake fiasco at lunchtime, my appetite had disappeared, but the smell of melted cheese and oregano had my stomach waking up and demanding attention.

"Are you sure?" I asked as I grabbed the blanket's soft fabric.

"Yep."

I shook it out and let it fall on Blake, who had stretched out on the couch. As soon as the blanket landed on his body, he flipped to his side, so he could prop my phone against the back of the couch. He snuggled in. Watching his body relax helped me relax.

I was exhausted but relieved.

With Blake situated, I moved into the kitchen to find Jackson cutting up the pizza. My mouth watered as he rolled the blade through the cheese and crust.

"Hungry?" he asked. His voice was low. I wasn't sure if he was teasing me or if he was genuinely interested in the state of my stomach.

"Starving," I whispered, deciding that if I wanted some food, being discreet wasn't the way to get it.

He chuckled, but then his gaze dropped down to my

shirt. It lingered there for a moment before his cheeks flushed, and he turned away from me.

That was strange. I pulled out my shirt, and my entire body heated from embarrassment. Somehow, I'd managed to get vomit all over me. How had I not noticed?

"Oh my gosh," I whispered. How had I not smelled this? What was I going to do?

Suddenly, Jackson was standing next to me. His hand was outstretched, and his fingertips brushed against my forearm. "Come with me. You can shower here, and I have some spare clothes for you to wear."

Trying to ignore the tingling on my skin, all I could do was nod. It was like his touch momentarily confounded me. I couldn't speak. I couldn't protest. All I could do was follow after him as he led me up to the loft and over to his bathroom.

He turned the water on, and as steam filled the room, he left me with a stack of fluffy white towels and a quick nod. As soon as the door was shut behind him, I collapsed against the counter.

A mixture of embarrassment and confusion coursed through me as I stared at my reflection in the mirror.

Something was happening to me. Something that felt both soul-crushing and exhilarating at the same time.

Jackson was changing. He was no longer the crabby, brooding man I'd met a few days ago. He was...caring.

And I wasn't sure how I felt about that.

THIRTEEN

Penny

---

*a*rcher had built a fire in the communal living room, and I figured it was the perfect place for me to plop down with my laptop and answer some emails. The smell of woodsmoke and the crackling flames filled me with a sort of peace that I hadn't felt in a long time.

I was still reveling in the feeling I got when Maggie chose the bouquet that looked like the one I had when I got married. That mixed with the nostalgia I felt when I sat across from Georgette reminiscing, and I was content.

A sensation that felt so foreign to me and yet was exactly what I needed.

I scanned through my emails, tapping the down button as I went. There were questions to be answered and fires to put out, but I wasn't in a hurry to answer any of them. Whatever needed to be solved would be solved.

If they couldn't get the answer from me, I was fairly certain that they would find it on their own.

The publishing world was vast and full of people who wanted to know more than the next. Everyone was scrambling to make it big. To prove their worth. It was an attitude that I was growing tired of.

Which brought my thoughts back to Georgette.

Would it be foolish to start over at *Magnolia Daily*? Would I be as happy there as I had once been? Would it fulfill me in a way that my current job didn't?

Was it the best move?

My stomach twisted at the thought. I wanted to be happy. I wanted to feel satisfied that what I was doing meant something. The longer I stayed at Sampson and Scotts, the more I was beginning to feel as if my soul was being sucked from my body.

I wasn't growing; I was stagnant.

It was an awful place to be.

"You look deep in thought."

I jumped slightly and glanced over to see that Maggie had sat down in the armchair next to me. She had a brown box in her lap and a soft smile on her lips. I must have looked panicked because she raised her hand in an apologetic manner.

"I'm so sorry. I didn't mean to startle you." She stood up.

I reached out and patted her hand. "You didn't startle me. I was lost in my thoughts, and it's a good thing you came around 'cause I needed to get out of them."

Maggie studied me for a moment before she moved to sit back down. "Anything I can help with?"

I wanted to talk to my daughter like a mother normally would. I wanted to tell her everything that was going on in my life. The good. The bad. But I wasn't sure how to do that. How did one climb that mountain? Did you just start talking and hope to get over your fear?

Did Maggie really want to know, or was she just being polite?

Not wanting to make a mistake in our relationship when things were going so well, I just smiled and then tapped on the box she was holding. "Is this for me?"

Maggie's expression faltered, but then she dropped her attention down to the box. I wondered for a moment if she felt disappointed in my reaction, but then I forced that from my mind. I was letting her guide this relationship. I wasn't going to push her into something she didn't want to do.

"It came this afternoon." She lifted it up slightly. "It's heavy."

I glanced at the address: New York. Recognition washed over me. "It's the books."

"Books?"

I nodded as I took the package off her lap and set it on the footrest in front of me. It took a minute for me to pick off the tape, but I finally got it removed enough to open the flaps. "Harper sent me advanced reader copies of the book I'm hoping you'll read for your book club."

I pulled out one of Jackson's books and couldn't help myself...I took a big whiff.

Then I felt embarrassed as I saw Maggie study me from the corner of her eye.

"Sorry," I mumbled as I set the book down next to the box. "Old habits, I guess."

Maggie's soft smile emerged as she shook her head. "No, I get it. I'm the same way with a new throw pillow or tapestry." She leaned into me. "If I buy one more pillow for my bed, Archer will call the wedding off."

I chuckled as I picked up the book again and let the soft texture of the cover slip over my fingers. "I guess that's something you got from me."

She quirked an eyebrow. "You have a lot of pillows?"

I nodded. "Pillows and books."

Maggie chuckled as she reached into the box and took out a book. She brought it to her nose and took in a deep breath. "I have to admit, that smells good."

A smile broke out across my lips as I watched my daughter mimic me. There was a strange sort of pride that filled my chest as I realized that, perhaps, Maggie and I were more similar than I'd thought.

"Right?" I said—a bit too loud. A guest who was sitting on the couch against the far wall cleared his throat and shot me a dirty look.

I pursed my lips after I mouthed an apology and then turned my attention back to Maggie. She looked as sheepish as I felt.

"Sorry," I whispered.

Maggie laughed as she shrugged. "It's okay. If he wants quiet, he should go to his room." Her voice was breathy as she leaned forward. I loved that she was snarky but only when the person couldn't hear her.

As much as I was labeled a witch in the publishing world, I honestly hated confrontation. I'd grown desensitized to it, but that didn't mean I actively sought it out. So I understood what Maggie was doing. Put that in the *similar attributes* column.

"So did you work with the author? Jackson Richards?" Maggie tapped the author's name on the cover and glanced up at me.

I nodded. "He's my best author. His books always become international best sellers."

She flipped through a few pages before she turned the book over and scanned the blurb. Then she nodded with her eyebrows raised. "Have you gotten anywhere with him?"

Maggie knew bits and pieces about Jackson and why I was here...but she didn't know everything. I wasn't sure if Jackson wanted this small town to know that much about him, but at this point, I honestly didn't care. If that man wanted privacy, he shouldn't have come to Magnolia. He shouldn't have run from me.

I needed to brainstorm ways of getting him to see things my way. To come to my side and reenter the publishing world. Whatever his issue was, we could face it together.

Running away was the last thing anyone should do. Problems always had a way of finding you.

Deciding to take a chance on my daughter—and knowing that she was as far from being a town busybody as one could get—I let her in. "I've gotten nowhere with him. That man is closed up tighter than a drum. I was hoping I could convince him with money or promises of success" —I blew out my breath— "but those didn't seem to tempt him."

When I was younger that concept would have seemed so foreign to me. After all, why wouldn't someone want money or fame? It was what I'd lived for. But now that I had all the money and prestige I could want, I saw things differently.

Relationships were what I valued now. Being a part of someone's life, having a place to go to on Christmas, those were the things I cared about. I'd ignored those things, and now I regretted making the choice to walk away.

I regretted leaving Maggie.

I swallowed against the lump in my throat. I glanced at my daughter for a moment—she looked as if she were chewing on my words—before I dropped my gaze. I wondered if she realized what I was thinking about. I wondered if she knew how much I regretted the things that I'd done. The moments in her life that I had missed.

The pit in my stomach began to widen as I thought about how a mother and daughter relationship should be. I should be able to admit my mistakes and apologize for them. We should have a relationship built on trust and honesty.

But we didn't.

And it was entirely my fault.

I parted my lips to speak. I wanted to tell her that I was sorry. That I had been wrong. But the words didn't come out. Maybe it was fear. Fear that I wouldn't say the right thing. Or that she wouldn't believe I was genuine. Fear that she wouldn't forgive me or that it wouldn't change anything.

Whatever the reason, I couldn't find the strength to speak. Instead, I just sat there with a slack jaw and a confused expression.

Maggie furrowed her brow. She blinked a few times before she leaned forward. "You okay?" she asked.

I quickly closed my lips and nodded. "Yeah," I said as I scrubbed my face and glanced around. I'd come so close to opening my heart up to Maggie. I'd almost put myself out there in a way I hadn't done in so long.

The fear that gripped me inside was dark and menacing. It took over my thoughts and my actions. It possessed me and kept me hidden. If I ever wanted to move past the relationship that Maggie and I currently had and create something more, I was going to have to beat this demon.

I was going to have to make a change.

But I couldn't do that. Not here. Not now.

"Sorry," I said after I shook my head. "I just spaced out there for a second."

Maggie looked skeptical but then quickly moved on. "So money and fame won't tempt the man…" Her voice drifted off like she was deep in thought. "What do you think he wants?"

I picked up the book that I had laid down and ran my fingers over the cover. It was buttery to the touch. "I don't know. Naomi and I tried to figure it out, too. She said that when Jackson got an idea in his head, it was hard to dissuade him." I sighed. "Which is aggravating."

Maggie nodded for a moment before the front doors to the inn opened, and a man dressed in a sheriff's uniform walked in. His hand was resting on his belt, and he took a look around as he removed his hat with his free hand.

When he spotted Maggie, he made his way over to us. Maggie was standing before I could even blink. I could tell that she was worried from the sudden tension in her shoulders.

"Sheriff," she said as she nodded.

"Hello, Ms. Brown. I got a call about a disturbance." He adjusted his stance. "Have you heard anything?"

Not wanting my daughter to deal with this alone, I quickly boxed the books back up and shoved my laptop into its bag.

"A disturbance? I'm not sure." She glanced around. "I haven't heard anything, and I've been here all day." She turned to look at me. "Did you hear anything?"

I shouldered my computer bag as I scooped up the

box of books. "Nothing." I glanced at the sheriff. "Did they say what it was about?"

Sheriff Morgan—his name was pinned to his left breast pocket—pulled out a small notebook. "Someone was complaining about a dog barking?"

Archer must have been alerted that something was going on. He appeared seconds after Sheriff Morgan finished speaking.

"We don't allow pets here," Archer said.

Sheriff Morgan flipped through his notepad. Then he cursed under his breath. "I'm so sorry. My new deputy is struggling. She said she swore that the person said Magnolia Inn, but I'm starting to think that they didn't." He scrubbed his face with his hand. "I'm thinking it's a mistake, but do you mind me looking around?"

Archer shook his head and extended his hand as he led the sheriff up the stairs and onto the second floor. I peeked over at Maggie to see that her face was still white and her expression grim.

"You okay?" I asked as I adjusted the book box so that I could reach out and pat her arm.

She glanced over at me and mustered a weak smile. "Yeah." Then she blew out her breath. "With this many guests, I know that a disturbance is to be expected. After all, it's the law of averages. But I guess I wasn't ready for that to happen just yet."

I moved over to the registration desk a few feet away and dropped my box behind it. Then I hid my computer behind some boxes of paper and rounded the desk once more.

Mom mode had kicked in. It felt strange and yet satisfying at the same time. Once I got back to Maggie, I wrapped my arm around her shoulders, led her toward the dining room, and sat her down at the nearest table.

While she waited, I hurried to gather a steaming hot mug of coffee and a cinnamon roll that was still warm. I set them down in front of her and then joined her at the table.

"I don't know why I was so startled by that," Maggie said, her voice breathy.

I gave her a soft smile. "This is your home. Your business. You don't ever want it defiled by people misbehaving." I scooted the mug of coffee closer to her until she picked it up and took a sip.

After a few more sips, the color began to return to her face. "Yeah. You're right." Then she brought up the back of her hand and pressed it to her cheek. "I feel so ridiculous."

I patted her hand resting on the table. She offered me a weak smile before she took in a deep breath. I kept quiet as she ate the cinnamon roll and sipped her coffee.

Even though neither of us spoke, there was a sort of calm that came from the silence between us. It was one that I hadn't ever felt.

My heart swelled at the thought of us growing closer. Was this what a mother and daughter relationship was? Was this what a family was?

Tears gathered under my eyelids as I fought to keep them from spilling.

Sitting here with Maggie, watching her eat and drink the food I brought over, I was beginning to realize one very important thing. I'd thought I was happy. I'd thought that I was satisfied with my life. I'd thought that all I needed was my career.

I'd thought wrong.

FOURTEEN

Fiona

---

*T*he water was warm as it beat down on me. I stood under Jackson's rainfall shower head, trying to piece together how I'd gotten here.

Blake had thrown up. Said throw-up had gotten on my shirt. Jackson had pointed it out to me and insisted that I use his bathroom to clean up. I let him.

Now I was standing here as steam filled the room, and I continued to feel as confused as ever.

Was this normal? I was fairly certain that this was not how housekeepers were treated. My job was simple— clean and cook. I was confused how him helping with my son or demanding I clean up in the exact shower I'd just washed fit within my job description.

I closed my eyes and let the water wash over my face. My muscles began to relax as I sunk into the warmth that surrounded me.

Even though I was confused, even though I was

worried what this all meant, the shower felt amazing. Maybe this was exactly what I needed in this moment.

So much of my life had been wrapped up in being a mom. Even when Blake was being watched by his grandmother, there was always a part of me that felt guilty. I should be the one to be with him. Bathe him. Dress him. Rock him to sleep.

I couldn't help but wonder if having a husband around—someone to love and care for Blake like I did—would mean more freedom for me. Freedom from the guilt that weighed down on me and never let me go.

Tears I didn't know I'd been holding back began to flow. Truth was, I felt sorry for myself. Sorry for the life I no longer had. Sorry for the stress that being a single mother put on me. Sorry for the fact that I felt so sorry for myself.

I was a mess. Even if I tried, it seemed as if I couldn't fix the situation I'd put myself into.

When I thought about planning for court, I felt like a glass vase, moments away from being pushed off the edge and shattered on the ground.

And if I broke, there was no way I was going to be able to be put back together again.

That was a scary thought. One that was hard to run from but easy to allow in to sit on your couch and take over you mind. Why was fear so much easier to live with than hope? Why was I more apt to doubt my ability than to find confidence in my strengths?

Was I ever going to feel comfortable in my life?

Not wanting to delve any deeper into my thoughts, I lathered up with soap, rinsed off, and got out of the shower. Once I was dry, I slipped on the clothes that Jackson had handed me and stared at my reflection.

It was ridiculous that a man who was as cold and confusing as Jackson would wear clothes that not only smelled good but were so soft and warm. How was that even possible?

I fingered the neckline for a moment, fighting the desire that grew inside of me until I couldn't hold it back anymore. I raised the hem of the shirt to my nose and inhaled. It smelled like sandalwood and laundry detergent.

It smelled like a man.

I hadn't been close to a man in too long. The scent. The warmth it gave my body. The fact that it had once been on Jackson's broad shoulders and muscled chest... well, it made my stomach flutter.

I allowed my thoughts to wander. What would it feel like to be touched by Jackson? To feel his heart beat through the thin fabric of his shirt. To smell him, raw and pure.

What would it feel like to have his lips on mine? Would he kiss me soft? Or hard?

I glanced at my reflection in the mirror. My fingertips made their way to my lips as I allowed my imagination to run wild. He seemed like the kind of man who would start out soft, hesitant. Then that kiss would move into something deeper and more meaningful.

My entire body burned for the sensation. I ached to be touched again. To be held again.

Three loud knocks on the door snapped me out of my daydream. I yelped and turned, yanking my hand down from my mouth and inwardly scolding myself for taking so long.

"Coming," I sang out as I hurriedly hung up the towel I had used and gathered my soiled clothes. With them tucked securely under my arm, I reached out and opened the door.

Jackson was standing on the other side. His expression was clouded, but the moment he saw me, his eyebrows went up. A small sense of joy rushed through me as I took in his reaction. I hadn't expected him to look so startled, but the fact that I could throw him off his guard…well, it felt amazing.

"I'm sorry I took so long. Is Blake okay?" I stepped closer to him, so I could peer outside the bathroom, but that brought me within inches of his body. He didn't seem in a hurry to step back.

Surprised, I glanced up at him only to see him staring down at me. His normally dark blue eyes had softened. My gaze ran down the planes of his face. I hadn't fully appreciated his features until now. Being this close, I could study them and wonder what it would feel like to run my hands across his cheekbones. To have his scruff rub against my own soft skin.

My heart picked up speed, so I cleared my throat, hoping to mask the sound.

"Blake?" he asked as if it had taken this long for him to register that I'd asked him a question. His voice was deep, and the tones had my body responding.

Not wanting to reveal what his presence was doing to me, I kept my lips pinched shut and nodded.

"He's fine. Still watching that show, snuggled on the couch." He waved his hand toward the living room.

"Oh." I frowned. "Did you need something?" And then I felt like an idiot. I stepped to one side of the bathroom doorway. "Did you need to use the facilities?"

Jackson's gaze drifted into the bathroom, and then he shook his head. "No. I just didn't want your pizza to get cold." Suddenly, a plate full of food appeared in front of me.

Not sure what else to do, I took it from him. My fingers brushed his during the exchange. It felt as if I'd touched lightning—if lightning was large and warm. My stomach did a little flip from the sensation, and my hands wanted to linger. To explore.

"Thanks," I said as I held up the plate.

Jackson pushed his hand through his hair. For a moment, his scar was exposed before his hair fell in front of it once more. He didn't seem alarmed that I'd seen it. In fact, he didn't take notice at all. His gaze shifted around the room before it landed back on me.

Was he trusting me? Was this a form of opening up?

My mind was whirling at the thought of what this meant. Did I dare hope that it meant something more?

Jackson studied me for a moment before he shook his

head and stepped to the side. "I'm an idiot," he murmured under his breath before he shot me a sheepish smile. "You probably don't want to eat in the bathroom. I didn't mean to cage you in."

I held the plate close—desperate to hang onto anything that would ground me—and shook my head. "Yeah, I'd rather eat at the table."

Jackson's little nods of acknowledgement were adorable. He looked completely out of his element as he stood there, hands in his front pockets, dark floppy hair shifting with the movement. "I figured."

I paused, waiting to see if he was going to lead the way. When he didn't move, I decided to take charge.

I went to check on Blake. When I discovered that he'd fallen asleep, I brushed his hair off his forehead and pressed my palm against it. He was warm, but not as warm as he had been earlier. I took that as a good sign. I hoped that meant Blake's fever was breaking.

After I tucked him in, I headed into the kitchen and found Jackson sitting at the dining table. He had a plate of food in front of him, and he was leaning back as if he wasn't ready to start eating. My heart fluttered.

He'd waited for me.

Not sure where to sit, I moved to sit on the seat in the corner.

"Oh."

I paused and glanced over at Jackson; he looked crestfallen.

"Is this not okay?" I asked as I picked my plate back up.

Jackson's cheeks hinted pink as he shook his head and motioned toward my chair. "No, no. It's fine. Go ahead."

I hesitated for a moment and then decided to just sit. This was ridiculous. He'd invited me to eat with him because he felt bad for me, not because we were on a date. I needed to remember that.

I needed to keep myself from slipping into a mental back-and-forth about his intentions. A lot had happened today, and it wasn't wise of me to start trying to interpret his little mannerisms. Not if I wanted to keep from embarrassing myself and losing my job.

The legs made a scraping noise as I pulled my chair closer to the table. I kept my gaze focused on the pizza in front of me and tried to ignore the silence that had engulfed the room. I kept my attention downward for a moment before I glanced up and caught Jackson staring at me.

He looked confused. Like he was looking for something but wasn't sure what he wanted to see. It made me feel vulnerable to be studied like that.

"Are you okay?" I asked as I took a bite of pizza. Just as the words left my lips, a piece of food flew to the back of my throat, throwing me into a coughing fit. It only lasted a minute, but it felt like an eternity. Thankfully, Jackson had set two glasses on the table, and while I was hacking away, he stood and set one next to my plate.

"You okay?" he asked, repeating the words that had got me into this mess.

I nodded, my eyes watering. "I'm fine," I wheezed out.

Suddenly, Jackson was in front of me, peering into my face once again as if he were looking for something. I felt paralyzed as he leaned in, running his gaze over my face. Part of me was completely wrapped up in the closeness of his body. The other part of me was panicked that he'd seen something and wanted to get a good look.

"I'm good, really," I whispered as I finally found the strength to lift up my hands and prove to him that I was going to be okay.

As if he suddenly realized how close he'd gotten to me, he pulled back. His shoulders dropped as he pushed his hair out of his face and hurried back over to his seat. As soon as he was situated, he started to eat as if he were the hungriest person in the world.

I studied him, trying to figure out what that was all about. But every time I opened my lips to speak, no words came out. I wanted to ask the question, but my body was actively keeping me from doing it.

Blast this self-preservation mode.

We ate in silence until Jackson said, "I'm sorry," so quietly that it was hard to hear. I had to lean in, and even then, I still feared that I hadn't heard him right.

"It's okay," I replied, hoping that he would realize I wasn't a foe. I wanted to be a friend, even if he reacted in strange ways. Even if my body eagerly responded to every motion he made to get closer to me.

He glanced up at me for a moment, and I was taken away by the intensity in his stare. It made my heart pound. I could see the pain that resided there, and I wanted to know more.

I needed to know more.

Deciding to take the plunge, I asked, "What made you move to Magnolia?"

He took a bite of crust and chewed thoughtfully. "Colten is here. That was a big selling point."

I wasn't really hungry anymore, but I also didn't want our conversation to stop. So I mindlessly picked off pieces of crust and slipped them into my mouth. "Have you guys been friends long?"

He nodded but didn't offer more.

Wanting to keep this conversation going, I decided to fill in the gaps myself. "You have to be good friends if you move to live near him. And you had to be doing well to be able to afford a fully furnished house on the beach." I waved to the covered windows. Even though I couldn't see it, the ocean's presence could be felt through the closed blinds.

He narrowed his eyes. "You're still trying to figure out what I do."

I shrugged. "I'm curious, that's all." My voice trailed off as I battled with myself over whether or not I should say what was on my mind. I decided to rip off the bandage. "You interest me."

Jackson didn't look startled. It took him a minute before his brows knit together and his gaze found my own. I could tell he was confused even if he was trying to fight that expression.

"I interest you?"

I wanted to say he interested me in more ways than one, but I wasn't sure how he would take it. And I wasn't sure if I could survive his response if it wasn't favorable. "I failed so much with my ex that I now second-guess every impression I have of men. I want to know more about you so that I can make a better assessment of your intentions." The words flowed out of me like water. It was almost impossible to rein them in once I started speaking.

I paused, waiting for his response. Did he think I was an idiot? Had I shared too much? Had I officially gone over the line you weren't supposed to cross with your boss?

We were friends, though, or so I thought. But his silence was deafening to me. Why wasn't he saying anything?

"You're worried about my intentions?" His voice was low, and I hated that I detected a hint of concern in it. Why was I allowing myself to read into everything? I shouldn't. I should stay far away from him.

"Yes," I whispered, knowing full well that staying away from people who weren't good for me wasn't one of my talents.

"Why?"

I took a bite of pizza to give myself time to decide how to answer his question. I wanted to be truthful. I wanted to tell him that my feelings for him were growing past that of housekeeper and house owner. He was doing things to me, and it was confusing me. I wanted to back away. I wanted to run. But I was starting to understand that responding that way wasn't an option for me anymore.

I was becoming too emotionally invested in him.

"I don't know," I finally responded. And that was truth. I didn't know anything anymore. I wasn't sure what I wanted, who I was, or what my future held.

All I knew was that I felt confused.

Jackson didn't respond to my weak confession. All he did was stare at me for a moment before dropping his gaze back down to the table. My entire face felt as if it were going to catch on fire. I wanted to take the words back. I wanted to have a do-over.

I wanted to get myself out of this mess.

But I wasn't sure how to do any of that while I sat paralyzed in my chair. I stared at the man who now knew I cared about him, or that I was at least interested in him.

A piercing sound broke the silence, and I straightened in my chair.

My phone.

I slipped it from the pocket I'd stashed it in and glanced down. *Austin.*

"I should go. This is my lawyer, and if he's calling

me, that's not good." I hurried to bring my plate to the sink.

"Oh," Jackson said, but I didn't wait to see if he had anything more to add.

I grabbed my bag of soiled clothes, my purse, and lastly my sleeping child. There were a few moments where one or all of the items I was clinging to felt as if they were going to slip, but I managed to keep ahold of them even if my fingers felt like they were going to break.

Jackson was standing by the table as I hurried past him to the front door. I almost dropped Blake but managed to keep ahold of him as I turned the handle and made my way out to my car.

On my way home, I called Austin. He told me that the judge was moving up our case to early next week. All I could do was agree, after all, did I have any other choice?

We hung up, the butterflies in my stomach dive-bombing the sides of my gut. Not only did I have to worry about my child support hearing, but I also needed to deal with what was happening between Jackson and me.

Or what *wasn't* happening. I still wasn't sure what was going on.

When I got to the coffee shop, Mom gave me an incredulous look as I passed by. I could tell that her expression was asking, *Whose clothes are these and why are you wearing them?*

But I didn't stop to talk. What I wanted was to get

upstairs, lay Blake down, and change out of Jackson's clothes.

Then I wanted to stick them in a bowl and hold a séance over them. I wanted to rid myself of all the feelings that were somersaulting in my stomach. Because with the way I was feeling, I was never going to be able to go back to Jackson's house. I was never going to be able to face him.

Even though I didn't want to admit it, I was fairly certain of one thing. I liked him.

I liked him a lot.

FIFTEEN

Fiona

$\mathcal{I}$ woke up just as jittery as when I went to bed the night before. My stomach was in knots, and I felt more confused than ever. I was hoping the feelings that had grown while I was with Jackson yesterday had just been part of a bad dream and I would wake up refreshed and calm and free of the attraction I felt for that man.

What a joke.

As I lay on my bed next to my sleeping child, staring up at the ceiling above me, I was just as infatuated and confused as when I collapsed into bed last night.

Rolling to my side, I hugged the body pillow I'd had to get when I was pregnant with Blake and sighed, burying my face into the soft fabric.

I felt like a teenage girl obsessing about her high school crush. Just thinking of Jackson's smile or the intensity in his eyes caused my emotions to stir, which was not a good sign.

Not when I had to work for the man day in and day out, at his house. In his presence. There was no way I was going to survive if this was the way I felt for him.

Inevitably, I was going to do something stupid. Inevitably, he was going to realize how I felt. Inevitably, I was going to end up jobless and right back where I'd been before I took this job.

I didn't have time for a crush, and I certainly didn't have time for the consequences of this particular crush. If I wanted what was best for my family—for Blake—then I needed to shut these feelings down *now* before they grew out of control.

Especially when I was fairly certain the feelings that I had for Jackson were one-sided. He saw me as his house-maid and the woman who brought her son over to throw up on his blankets.

Other than that, I wasn't anything to him, much less a romantic interest.

I groaned as I buried my face into my pillow and whisper-screamed into the down fill.

I was a mess, plain and simple.

Once I'd calmed down from my freak-out session, I flipped to my back and sighed. If I tried hard enough, I could forget my blossoming feelings for Jackson—I could. I just needed self-control and determination. Both things that came along with being a mother.

I was going to win this struggle no matter what.

Feeling hopelessly optimistic that I could accomplish the task I'd set out for myself, I grabbed my phone off my nightstand and punched in my passcode. I had about ten more minutes before I needed to get up and get ready to go, so I was going to spend those minutes mindlessly checking social media.

Just as my phone lit up, I noticed that I had a missed text message. My heart picked up speed when I saw who it was from…Jackson.

In a matter of seconds, all of my determination flew right out the window. I was back to being a ditz— complete with butterflies in my stomach and sweaty palms.

Gah! A minute into my goal and I'd already thrown it out the window.

This was going to be a long process.

I had no energy to fight the feelings that arose, so I decided to just see what Jackson sent. If my hands were shaking and my head felt woozy, I was just going to lean into it. After all, what other option did I have?

Jackson: Bring your swimsuit today. And if you have Blake again, bring his as well.

I sat up on my bed, holding the covers to my chest for warmth. I leaned forward to stare at the screen once more. Did he say what I thought he said?

I scanned over his message once more. Yep. He wanted to take me and Blake swimming.

Where? Outside? What about his hatred of light? I was fairly certain that Jackson never left his house, and being a new resident, how would he know where to take us?

And why us?

I was trying to feel indifferent about this guy, and he went ahead and invited me *and my son* to go swimming. Did that mean he cared about Blake?

Did I want him to?

My heart was racing now as I clutched my phone in my hands. My thumbs were poised to type, but I wasn't sure what to say. Did I ask him if it was a joke? Did I tell him that Blake and I couldn't go?

Did I quit?

I felt like a jumble of nerves and decided to throw caution to the wind and just respond. After all, I was trying to trust my gut more. What better place to start than here?

Before I could stop myself, I started typing.

Me: Sounds good. It might just be me. I'll see how Blake is when he wakes up.

Then I tossed my phone back onto the nightstand and stood. There was no way I could relax now.

I was going to shower, eat breakfast, get Blake ready, and leave before I would allow myself to check and see if he responded.

If I was going to spend my afternoon in a swimsuit with Jackson, then I needed to prove to myself that I had self-control. I needed to prove I could keep my impulses in check.

It was torture, moving around my phone all morning

but not allowing myself to pick it up. I was acutely aware of it at all times, and I had to mentally force myself to stop *"accidentally"* knocking it over so that I could get a glimpse of my notifications.

I might be losing my mind.

Blake, on the other hand, seemed completely fine. He woke up bright-eyed and smiley—a stark contrast to the day before. If I hadn't witnessed his vomiting sessions, I would have never guessed that he'd been sick as a dog yesterday.

I envied my son's ability to snap back so quickly.

Deciding that he might still be infectious, I dressed Blake in his beach clothes. I figured that Bonnie would be happy if I kept him home another day, and I wanted to see how Jackson would react to hyper, non-pukey Blake.

I was fairly certain he wouldn't have the patience for it. And that would solve the conundrum I'd found myself in. If Jackson couldn't handle my child, then a relationship with him wasn't an idea I was going to entertain. My feelings would stop right where they were.

Mom raised her eyebrows when I came out of my room with Blake trailing behind me. She was still confused as to what had happened last night, but I really wasn't ready to talk about it. After all, Mom had a way of reading me, and I wasn't sure I wanted her to know that I was beginning to have feelings for my boss.

I offered her a quick smile before I got started on breakfast. After I poured Blake's sugary cereal, I set him up at the table with a spoon, and he dove in. I wasn't in the mood to cook anything right now. Not when I felt so distracted.

Once my mug was full of coffee, I turned to give my attention to Mom. She was daintily eating a piece of raisin bread with an incredulous expression.

I'd never felt so judged.

"Blake threw up at Jackson's, and I needed a change of clothes," I blurted out before I could stop myself.

Mom's eyebrows rose as she took another bite of her toast.

"What was I supposed to do? Wear my thrown up on clothes?" I waved toward my shirt. Why wasn't she talking? What was she thinking?

"There's nothing going on between us. I work for him, and that's it." I brought my mug to my lips. If I was drinking, I wasn't talking. I was spilling way more than I'd intended, and Mom hadn't even uttered a syllable.

A few seconds ticked by before Mom set her toast back down on her plate and brushed off her fingertips. Then she took a long drink of her milk. I'd never realized how annoying my mother could be until right now.

I was dying, and she was enjoying herself.

"That was a lot of information to process at once," she said, her stoic expression shifting to one of amusement.

I huffed and turned away from her, so I could grab the bread and toast myself a slice. "I'm glad my pain is your enjoyment."

Mom chuckled. "You seem to be fairly flustered by this man."

Heat pricked at my skin. I'd known she was going to be able to read me, but I'd kind of hoped that she wouldn't be so direct with her words. They caught me off guard, and it was strange to hear them linger in the air because there was truth to them.

I *was* flustered by Jackson.

In fact, *flustered* was underselling it. I was completely confused by the man. I'd hoped that when I got home and climbed into bed, I would forget those feelings. But that hadn't happened.

Not in the least.

And now I was here, fully awake, feeling more confused than ever.

"Do you have feelings for him?" Mom's voice had grown serious. I glanced over my shoulder to see her leaning in. Her brows were furrowed, and I could tell she was concerned—which only made me feel worse.

"I don't know," I whispered as I pulled out my piece of toast and began to butter it. Even though I knew I was lying, I wasn't ready to face the truth. The truth left me vulnerable, and I was still trying to address the last thing that had torn down my walls.

I wasn't in a place to start anything new. Not until I fixed my past with Dave. I was in the middle of a child support battle. Introducing a new man into my life was foolish.

It wasn't part of my plan.

Mom's crease between her brows deepened, which only made me feel worse. She was worried about me, and if I didn't address it now, her previous feelings were going to emerge. Mom had always worried about my relationship with Dave, and I didn't want her to think I was headed down the same path now.

I'd grown. I'd changed. I wasn't going to dive head-first into a new relationship and let it take over me.

I took a bite of my toast and chewed. This whole conversation was pointless anyway. This was only my interpretation of events. There was a good chance that Jackson was just a nice guy and had no intention of wanting anything more.

I was assuming that he wanted to date me. That I was more to him than just his housekeeper. For all I knew, our relationship was completely innocent, and I was the only one reading into this.

Which would make me a fool.

"It's going to be fine. I may have some feelings for him, but I don't think that they're reciprocated. He's got his life. I've got mine." I shoved the rest of my toast into my mouth and gave my mom a strained smile. Blake had finished his breakfast and wandered out into the living room. I grabbed my purse and slipped my feet into my sandals before heading after him.

I located Blake's shoes and hunched over him to slip them on. I heard the sound of chair legs scraping against the floor, and a moment later, Mom was standing over me. I could feel the words that she wanted to say.

She had another lecture to deliver.

I swallowed the last bits of my toast as I slipped Blake's shoes on and then stood. Mom parted her lips, but I stopped her before she said anything.

I was confused and hurting—there was no need to drive that nail home. "I won't do anything. I'm just working there." I reached over and wrapped my arm around her shoulders. I wanted her to stop. I couldn't handle this right now.

When I pulled back, Mom's lips were closed, but I could tell that she still wanted to say something. I hated that she didn't trust me. That I'd caused her to worry like this. She deserved better.

"I'll be fine," I said with a soft smile. Then I turned to open the door. Blake wandered out with his sippy cup in one hand and a teddy in the other. Knowing I couldn't let him be out there for long, I walked through the doorway before I turned and nodded. "I'll see you tonight."

Mom had wrapped her left arm across her chest and was resting the elbow of her right arm on it. She was tapping her chin, and I could see the words that she was stopping herself from saying.

She hesitated before she nodded. "Be safe."

I grabbed ahold of the door handle and pulled. With the door now shut, I let out my breath as my confidence began to waver.

Mom doubted my ability to keep my feelings in check, which only made me feel weak. My focus should be on Blake and my relationship with Dave—I knew this. But she didn't know just how strong my feelings for Jackson were. Or how he made me feel.

When I was around him, I felt different. I felt special.

I felt like Fiona. Not a mom or a single woman.

Jackson made me feel different.

But Mom's reservations were well-founded, and I couldn't risk my son's happiness. If I allowed Jackson into my life only to have him leave, that would crush my son's heart and mine at the same time. I couldn't risk that.

Not when we were so broken already.

I didn't want to admit it, but Mom was right to worry. If I was going to survive my future, then I needed to let go of my past self.

Even though Jackson made me feel like a woman again, pursuing that was something past Fiona would have done. Present Fiona needed to protect herself, and the only way to do that was by saying no to my desires.

Even if my desire was a tall, brooding man.

SIXTEEN

Penny

$\mathscr{M}$ aggie seemed to be in better spirits today. Perhaps it was because Colten discovered that the source of the disturbance was just a kid watching cat videos on YouTube a bit too loud. Or maybe it was because the sun was shining, and she'd opened the windows to let in the salty air.

I wanted to think that she was in a better mood because of the bonding moment we shared yesterday.

The truth was, *I* felt closer to her. Closer than I'd felt in a long time.

As strange as it was to say, I was beginning to feel complete. A sensation that I wasn't sure I'd ever felt fully. Or at least, I hadn't felt it in a long time. I was beginning to realize that my daughter had been the source both times.

I adjusted my readers on my nose as I walked into the dining room and sat down in the far corner. Brett had made scones, and they were the centerpiece on each table. I liked that the food was right on the table, and, not feeling the need to get up for more, I pulled a scone out of the basket and sat back to enjoy it.

It was a cranberry and lemon scone, and it tasted divine. I pulled off chunks and slipped them into my mouth while I stared out at the ocean that spanned the horizon. The sun was up and reflected off the blue water. The ambiance and view had all of my stress melting away.

"Well, you look like you are in a good mood," Maggie said as she draped a dish towel over her shoulder and sat down next to me. Her hair was pulled back into a bun, but small wisps still framed her face.

For the first time, I had a desire to tuck them behind her ear—but then decided against it. She was my daughter, not a toddler. Even though I missed those years, that didn't mean she would appreciate me attempting to go back to that time.

"I am," I said, letting my breath out with a sigh. I enjoyed consistently waking up in a good mood. It was definitely something I could get used to. Which only made me think harder about what Georgette had said.

The desire to take her up on her offer grew stronger by the moment. This could be my life. Living by the ocean. Being by my daughter. And once she married Archer, I was fairly certain grandkids were in my future.

Could I be happy with this life?

I wanted to believe that I could.

"Georgette asked me to come run *Magnolia Daily*," I blurted out before I could stop myself. It was partly from my excitement, but I also wanted to gauge Maggie's reaction. How would she feel about me staying permanently? Would she feel like I was stepping on her toes?

Her reaction wasn't really what I expected. It was quiet and reserved. Her eyebrows were raised, and her lips parted. She looked more shocked than excited. My heart sank.

My daughter didn't want me here. Of course she didn't. Her response was a polite one, but I could tell this was not what she wanted. I didn't blame her.

After all, I'd been a source of pain for so long, and I was a fool to think that she would actively welcome me into her life after I'd treated her the way I did.

She was being nice because I was only here for a short time. I doubted she would do the same if I were here for good.

"I turned it down, of course," I hurried to say. There was no way I wanted to put myself out there like that. Not when my heart could be pulled from my chest and pulverized. I was already living in fear of losing my career. I couldn't put my relationship with my daughter —as pathetic as it was—on the line as well.

"Oh, you did?" Maggie asked. Her voice was even more hushed.

I must have really startled her, and I felt like a terrible mom because of it. "Yes. I mean, I've worked so hard for Sampson and Scotts. It would be foolish to leave now."

Why had I even said anything? Why had I tested the waters like that?

"Yeah, I see your point."

I reached out to pat her hand, but just as I hovered over it, I changed my mind and made a beeline for the scone basket. It left me with two scones, but I had to stop acting like my relationship with Maggie was fixed.

It wasn't.

It was going to take a lot more time and a lot more effort for me to get her to trust me again.

I needed to let her guide me instead of plowing ahead with my desires like I'd done in the past.

Needing something to do, I shoveled the scone into my mouth. Maggie seemed to be in a daze. Her cheery demeanor had disappeared, replaced with a grey cloud.

My stomach felt like lead. I hadn't realized how much she didn't want me here in Magnolia or how much that thought would darken the relationship between us. Here I was, thinking that things were getting better, only to discover I was wrong.

Terribly wrong.

Just then, my phone rang. It could have been Satan himself calling me and I'd have sung hallelujah. I needed a reason to pull the cord on this conversation and get out of here.

Even though the scone felt like paste in my mouth, I pulled my phone out. I shot Maggie an apologetic smile and hurried to the hallway, where I brought the phone to my cheek.

If I was excusing myself to take a call, I was going to need to actually take the call. I didn't want Maggie to think that I was abandoning her once more.

Even though, through my stupidity, that was exactly what I was doing.

"Hello?" I asked, not bothering to look at who was calling.

"Penny?"

"Mr. Sampson." I'd recognize his nasally voice anywhere.

"Good. We've been trying to contact you the last few days, but you haven't answered."

I wanted to tell him it was because I was avoiding him, but that wouldn't put me back in his good graces. After all, I needed this job. The whole idea of staying in Magnolia had just been shot down by my daughter. If I didn't want to be homeless, I needed to focus and get my career back in gear.

"I'm so sorry. Reception can be spotty on this island." That was a half-truth, but he didn't need to know that.

"Ah, I see."

I doubted that he did. A man living in a penthouse in New York knew nothing about spotty internet.

I shushed the snarky comments filling my mind and forced myself to focus. Even though my heart was pounding in my chest from the conversation I'd had with Maggie, I needed to focus if I was going to save my job.

My internal stamina and grit when things were going

horribly wrong were my super powers. And I was going to channel that trait with all the strength I could muster.

"If you're calling to check in on Jackson and me, I'm happy to report that things are progressing. We're in talks about how to resolve his concerns so that he can rejoin the *'family.'* " Ugh, that word tasted vile as it came out of my mouth.

We weren't a family—even if I was struggling with the definition of that word in my own life. Sampson and Scotts was a cutthroat, dog-eat-dog company. I may not know what family meant, but I knew it wasn't that.

Even though Maggie may be reserved around me, I knew that she still cared about my well-being. She still wanted what was best for me. We weren't a perfect family, but we had basic decency down, that I did know.

The basics were a foundation on which to build our future. That was what I was determined to do no matter how many times I'd made a mess of things. I was always going to be able to go back to the start.

I couldn't see Sampson and Scotts offering the same grace to Jackson.

Mr. Sampson cleared his throat. I wasn't sure if it was because he was disappointed with my work or if the word *family* caused the same reaction in him as it had in me.

"Well, I'm glad that things are moving forward. Though it would be inaccurate to say we're not disappointed things aren't progressing faster. But if you're confident that things will return to normal in the next week, then I can guarantee that we'll hold your job."

My mouth turned dry. One week or I'd lose my job? How was that fair? But then I shoved that thought from my mind. Sampson and Scotts didn't care about fairness or loyalty. They cared about results. And if I wanted to continue in this company, I was going to have to provide results.

"I understand." I managed a professional tone—thank goodness. He didn't need to know that I was close to breaking. I honestly doubted he would even care.

"Good. I hope to see you in a week with his written agreement in hand and a timeline of how we are going to move forward. If not…" He ended with a click of his tongue.

Great. He'd repeated himself, so I fully understood what he meant. Like I was child being reprimanded by my father.

"I will be there," I promised and then pulled the phone from my cheek. I wasn't sure if he wanted to keep going with this conversation, but I didn't want to take that ride with him. So I hung up and turned my focus to what I was here to do.

Get Jackson.

Maggie had moved from the table by the time I turned back to the dining room. Not wanting to revisit how much my daughter hated the idea of me living here, I hurried up to my room and shut the door.

Silence engulfed my room as I stood in the entryway. Hot tears pricked at my eyes, and I wanted to let them fall. I wasn't a big crier, though there were times in my life when they'd threatened to spill.

Crying would only make me feel weaker. It would exhaust my resolve to fix what Jackson had broken. If I was going to meet him with guns blazing, I needed to be firing on all eight of my take-no-crap cylinders.

Otherwise, he would see right through me.

I quickly showered and dressed in my freshly pressed pantsuit. Maggie had sent Archer up to my room to collect my dry cleaning a few days ago. He'd looked less than thrilled, but I thanked him and got a grunt in response.

Yesterday, when I got back to my room, my clothes had been placed on my bed—still in their dry cleaner's bags.

While I hung up the clothes in my closet last night, I'd contemplated inviting Maggie and Archer out to dinner. But now, in light of how Maggie felt about me and my presence here, I decided that would be a very bad idea.

Maggie was ready for me to go home. And if I were honest with myself, I was ready too. After all, I wasn't a small-town girl. I lived and breathed New York City. The smells, the noise, the constant movement of people through the streets—that was my life.

To think that I could settle down and run a small newspaper was downright laughable. I could see the headlines:

Big-City Editor Tries to Make it as Small-Town Reporter and FAILS!

Because that is what I would do—fail.

I brushed on my makeup and styled my hair in a low bun. I was going to be fierce. I wanted Jackson to know that I wasn't going to take no for an answer and needed to make sure I looked the part.

I collected my purse and slipped on my shoes. Once I was ready, I locked my door and headed downstairs.

Maggie was standing at the receptionist desk with the phone propped between her cheek and shoulder. Her eyes widened when she saw me, but I just shot her a quick wave before I pushed through the front door and out into the hot afternoon air.

The drive to Jackson's house was quiet. I decided to focus on what I was going to say instead of replaying what had happened with Maggie over and over in my mind. After all, it solved nothing and only made me more agitated.

I parked behind his house and got out. A part of me feared what would happen when I knocked on the door.

SEVENTEEN

Fiona

*J*ackson was in a good mood. When he answered the door, he was wearing a multicolored pair of swim trunks, a white sleeveless tee, a baseball hat, and a dark pair of sunglasses. His smile was hard to ignore, and when he dropped down to say hi to Blake, I about lost my mind.

He wasn't being fair. If he was just my friend, why was he acting this way? Was I ever going to be able to go back to normal life? Would I ever go back to a time when I was just his employee, and not the girl who was beginning to fall for him?

My assessment of my feelings for him had been wrong. I'd lied to Mom just like I had lied to myself. I liked Jackson.

I liked him a lot.

"Ready to go?" he asked when he popped back up. He and Blake were working on a secret handshake which took a minute to get all the way through. Especially when Blake was struggling to keep up.

I pinched my lips together as I swallowed my feelings. I needed to keep a level head. As long as my desires stayed just that—desires—then I was going to be fine. I just needed to make sure that I never acted on them.

"We're ready," I whispered when Jackson furrowed his brow. Apparently, my silence was alarming to him.

He clapped his hands together. "Perfect." Then he disappeared inside for a moment and reappeared with a few lawn chairs slung over his shoulder and a blanket draped over his arm. "I had Colten grab us some food from town," he said as he lifted the basket into the air.

I smiled and nodded as I wiggled my hand into Blake's. Jackson shut the door behind him, and we were now standing on his porch, just the three of us.

The three of us.

I hated that we felt like a family. It was ridiculous to even allow myself to think like that. We weren't a family, and we were never going to be. That word should be struck from my vocabulary.

"I found the perfect spot. It's only, like, a ten-minute walk." Jackson's grin widened. "Does that sound okay?"

I nodded. Blake didn't wait for us. Instead, he slipped his hand out of mine and took off toward the sand. That seemed to bolster Jackson as he hurried after him. I took my time crossing the porch and walking down the stairs to the sand. Once I got there, I slipped my shoes off and held them so that they dangled from my fingertips.

I kept a few feet behind Jackson, who was walking with Blake along the water's edge. Every so often, a wave would wash just high enough to cover Blake's feet. He'd scream with delight and take off toward the water only to be pulled back by Jackson. They'd laugh and continue walking only to have it happen again.

I tried to ignore how I felt while watching this man interact with my son. I tried to remain platonic. I tried to keep my feelings at bay. But it was impossible.

This man was impossible.

Here I was, trying to keep myself from falling for this man only to have him sweep me away with his care of my son. He clearly wanted to have a relationship with Blake. There was no requirement, no expectation for him to act this way at all—and, well, it made me melt.

Why was I so weak?

When we got to the perfect spot, Jackson set up the lawn chairs. He dusted off one of the seats and then motioned toward it. "M'lady," he said with a deep bow.

Not sure how to react, I just smiled and sat. If I was going to pretend that I wasn't attracted to him, sitting in a seat that he set up for me was part of that charade.

If I refused, that would mean I thought his gesture meant something. But sitting would prove that I didn't think he meant anything by it.

My rationale was confusing, but it was keeping me sane. And right now, that was all I could ask of myself.

I sat while Blake and Jackson played by the water. They built a sandcastle, picked up shells, and Jackson even let Blake bury him in the sand. They seemed in heaven while I sat on the chair, watching. I wanted to join in—it looked like so much fun—but I knew the moment I opened my heart up to the idea of us, I was going to fall. Hard.

And I wasn't ready for the nuclear fallout.

So I stayed back, watching and waiting for Blake to get tired so that we could go back to the house. Then I could return to my job as housekeeper, and Jackson could go back to his role as the cranky homeowner, and we could forget this whole ordeal. I wanted to go back to a time when my only worry was what I was going to do about Dave.

Instead, I was completely confused by two different men, and I wanted to stick my head in the sand and never come out.

How had my life come to this?

"Thirsty, Mommy," Blake said as he came running up to me. His hands were covered in sand, and his cheeks were pink from exertion and the sun.

I nodded and pulled open my beach bag and fished around until I found a juice box that I'd shoved in there. I inserted the straw and handed it over. Blake took it and hurried back over to his hole he'd been digging.

I stretched out my legs and swept the shore to locate Jackson, but I didn't find him. Not until he plopped down on the beach towel next to me and laid his head back.

"Tired?" I asked.

Jackson brought his ankle up to rest on his knee and

wiggled his foot a few times. Then he nodded. "It's a good tired."

I fished around for a water bottle. Once I cracked the lid, I offered it to him. When Jackson didn't take it right away, I tapped his foot with my finger. He startled and sat up, bringing him inches away from me. I hadn't realized I was leaning over him until I was met with my reflection in his sunglasses.

Heat raced to my cheeks as I stared at the black glass. I couldn't see his eyes, so I had no idea what he was thinking. It unnerved me.

I pulled back and settled into my chair. I needed a safe place; being that close to Jackson left me feeling raw and open.

"Thanks," he said, accepting the water bottle and taking a long drink.

"Of course," I managed to get out.

He leaned back on one arm and continued drinking.

I had so many questions floating around in my mind, and yet I couldn't find a way to ask any of them. Why did he bring us here? I thought he didn't like sunlight. What was his story? Was I ever going to find out?

"There's nothing more deafening than a question not asked."

I glanced over at him to see that his attention was cast forward. Was he talking to me?

"Huh?" I eloquently asked.

He turned to face me. "You have questions. I can see

them in your eyes." He took a sip of water. "It's deaf-ening that you aren't saying them."

I pinched my lips together, embarrassed that I'd found yet another person who could read me like a book. Why couldn't I be stealthier?

"I don't have questions," I mumbled before I closed my mouth again. I sounded so unsure that I didn't even believe me.

"Mm-hmm," he responded as he took another sip.

I knew that I was going to explode if I didn't ask my questions. Plus, working for him would be torture if I didn't determine where we stood. I needed to know his thoughts. And since he wasn't very forthcoming with them, I needed to seize on this opportunity and ask.

The worst thing he could do was fire me, and right now, I was seconds away from quitting. I was an emotional mess. Being confused and distracted was the last thing I needed. No matter how much he paid me.

"I thought you didn't like the sun." I pinched my lips together, hoping that I hadn't been too direct. But I wanted to know. I'd almost quit over how he treated me when I opened the blinds.

Jackson glanced over at me, his brows furrowed. I couldn't tell if he was angry or if he was trying to figure out why this was the topic I chose to bring up. His silence was stifling as I waited for him to respond.

"I don't dislike the sun," he said as he brought his knees up and wrapped an arm around them. His gaze had returned to the ocean, and his expression softened as he studied the water. "It's more like it doesn't like me." His voice drifted off with each word, and I had to lean closer for fear that I wouldn't hear what he had to say.

"It doesn't like you?" What did that mean?

Jackson scoffed and shook his head. "Let's just say that I don't like it to surprise me. When I'm outside, I can prepare for it." He tipped his face toward me. "When you opened the blinds, it surprised me. I was caught off guard."

I frowned. I felt more confused than ever. "You like to be prepared for the sun? Why?"

Jackson looked as if he were chewing on my words. Then he shrugged. "I have issues."

Yet again, he was evading my questions. "Everyone has issues," I muttered as I wiggled my toes deeper in the sand beneath my feet.

"Even you?"

I scoffed and nodded. "You have no idea."

I suddenly had Jackson's full attention. Instead of letting his gaze drift back to the water, he turned his body so that I was the only thing he was staring at. It was both unnerving and exhilarating at the same time. It had been so long since a man had studied me the way Jackson did.

It made me wonder, did he like what he saw?

"Blake's dad?"

His words were forthright and to the point. My heart picked up speed as I contemplated the question. I wanted to be open and honest. After all, Jackson was quickly becoming a part of my life. But I feared what would happen to me if I let him in. I'd been hurt so much in the past—was pain a part of my destiny?

"He left me and Blake alone." I decided to throw away my fears and be vulnerable. What else did I have to lose?

"Jerk," he mumbled under his breath.

That caused a smile to tug on my lips. It was nice when people took my side. I'd gotten so used to Dave telling me that I was wrong, that it was vindicating when people sided with me.

"Yeah, he was—is."

"Is?"

I nodded as I stretched my arms in front of me and curved my back. "He refuses to pay child support. I'm taking him to court..." My voice drifted off. The thought of standing in front of a judge terrified me. Even though Austin had assured me that I would win, that didn't stop the butterflies from assaulting my stomach.

There was so much at risk, and I didn't want to lose everything that I'd built for me and Blake. Magnolia had become Blake's entire world. If I was forced to take him from here, or worse, if Dave got custody of Blake, I would crumble. My entire world was wrapped around that little boy.

Suddenly, a hand appeared in my line of sight. I froze as I watched Jackson wrap his fingers around my hand and squeeze it. Electricity rushed through me at his touch. It was warm and tight and...exactly what I needed.

I let my gaze linger on our hands before glancing up at him. His lips were stoic, and for a moment, I wished I could see his eyes behind his sunglasses. I wanted to escape in his gaze. He made me feel at peace and scared at the same time. The fear wasn't about what he would do to me—but that I might fall for him and never get back up.

I was afraid that he would never feel the same for me, and I'd end up how fate wanted me to be all along —alone.

"I'm sorry that you are going through that. I watched my mom do the same. If there's anything I can do to help, just let me know."

I swallowed at his words. There was a tone to his voice that felt like hot chocolate to my ears. It was warm and comforting. I wanted to believe that he would be there for me no matter what. But the doubt inside of me was stronger than any words of confidence could be. He said he'd be there, but the moment it became hard, he would leave.

They always did.

"Thanks," I whispered as I allowed my gaze to drop to our hands once more. He hadn't pulled away, and I was desperate to know what that meant. Was it possible that he had feelings for me as well?

"Mommy!" Blake's shout had both of us whipping our gaze in his direction. He was standing over the hole he was digging and pointing to something inside of it.

Needing a break from Jackson's touch, I wiggled my

hand free and walked over to Blake. He was extremely proud of the hole he'd dug. I took the next hour to play with my son. We raced the waves, built another sandcastle, and picked up more seashells.

Jackson stayed on the blanket, and because of the darkness of his sunglasses, I wasn't sure if he was looking at us or sleeping. Even though I wanted to think that he was watching us, I knew better. He didn't have feelings for me. He was just a nice guy, that was all.

I was only going to get myself in trouble if I allowed myself to think any different.

Blake started to slow down, so I took that as a sign he was ready to go inside. I ushered him toward the blanket and chairs despite his protests. Jackson and I packed up our stuff and headed toward his house. Blake was dragging on the way back, so Jackson set down the things he was carrying and picked up Blake in one swoop. Suddenly, we were walking down the beach just like a family in a Hallmark movie.

It hurt my heart.

This was what Blake needed. A dad in his life that was going to play with him and then carry him to the car when he was too tired. All Blake had was me, and I felt as if I were failing him with everything I did.

Asking Dave to come back into his life wouldn't fix anything. Dave didn't want to be there to take him to T-ball games or tuck him in bed. Sure, Dave was going to eventually pay child support, but that was all I was going to get.

At the end of the day, Blake needed more. And there was no way I was going to be able to fill the hole that I knew was growing inside of my little boy.

By the time we got back to Jackson's house and laid Blake down on the couch, I'd worked myself up. I was angry that Dave wasn't a part of his son's life. I was angry that I couldn't be everything that Blake needed. But most of all, I was angry that Jackson was giving me a glimpse of something I wanted more than anything in the world, but it didn't mean anything. He wasn't a part of our life like Blake needed him to be, and yet he was fulfilling that role. He was giving us a taste of what we wanted without the commitment.

It wasn't fair.

I stood in the kitchen, fuming. I was so confused and agitated that I was going to explode. My mind was racing with everything that I wanted to say to Jackson—to men in general. I was tired of wanting something I was certain I could never have.

Jackson rounded the corner a few minutes later. He looked tired as he set his sunglasses down on the counter and turned to face me. His hair was pulled back, exposing his scar. It was strange that he wasn't even trying to hide it anymore.

"Blake's asleep," he said as he moved to the fridge and pulled out a beer.

Jackson's relaxed demeanor helped lessen the stress I felt on my nerves, but it didn't take it away entirely. My situation hadn't changed; I had to remember that.

"What do you want from me?" I blurted out before I could stop myself.

Jackson straightened and shut the fridge door behind him. Then he turned to face me. "What?"

I'd already gone this far, I might as well keep going. "What do you want from me and Blake? You're taking us to the beach. Taking care of my son when he's sick. Carrying him when he's too tired to walk." I was shouting now. I knew I should stop, but I didn't know how.

Jackson was staring at me. I was certain that I looked crazed, but I didn't care. He was frustrating me, and he needed to stop. Then his expression changed, and suddenly he was facing me head-on. Which startled me. What did he have to be stubborn about?

"Do you want to know?" he asked, stepping closer to me.

My heart stuttered as he neared. My confidence wavered as he towered over me. There was something in his gaze. Something that sent a siren off in my mind. I needed to back away. Something was going to shift in our relationship if we continued down this path.

But I was frozen. Partly because I was too stubborn to move. Partly because I wanted to know if he was implying what I thought he was implying.

"Yes," I whispered, unable to stop myself.

His hand went around my waist as he pulled me to him. Before I could think—before I could act—his lips were on mine.

EIGHTEEN

Fiona

The drumming of my heart drowned out the warning bells going off in my head. Even though I knew I needed to pull away, the truth was...I didn't want to. I wanted to kiss Jackson.

I wanted to feel his shoulders, his neck, and the tufts of his hair under my fingertips.

I tightened my grip on his neck as I pulled his lips closer to mine. It felt as if he were pulling me away, and I didn't want this to stop.

Not now.

He chuckled softly against my lips as he tightened his grip on my waist. Suddenly, I was airborne as he brought me up to sit on the counter. Fearing that he would leave, I wrapped my legs around his waist and pinned him there.

He kept one hand tight around my waist as he brought his other hand up to cradle my cheek. Our lips parted as we fell into a dance. It was as if we knew what the other wanted without either of us saying anything.

I wanted him, and he wanted me.

I wasn't sure how long we kissed, and I didn't care. It had been so long since I'd been held by a man—touched by a man—that I could stay here forever. Every part of me warmed at his touch, and I knew the minute he pulled away, the cloud I was perched on would disappear, and I would be alone, again.

My lips were throbbing when Jackson finally pulled back. I didn't want to let him go, so I kept my arms around him. He chuckled as he tipped his head forward and rested his forehead on mine.

"You okay?" he asked.

I pinched my lips together, remembering the feeling of his lips on mine. "Yes," I whispered.

His frowned as he studied me. Hating that he looked so concerned, I reached up to rub the crease between his brows.

"I'm fine."

He stared at me for a moment before he leaned in and pressed his lips to the tip of my nose. "Good. Because I've been wanting to do that for a long time."

Butterflies took flight in my stomach. I was fairly certain that my cheeks were pink because they felt on fire. "Really?" Suddenly, I was a high schooler who just found out that the popular guy liked her.

Jackson nodded as he tucked my hair behind my ear. "You have no idea," he growled as he wrapped his arm around my waist once more and pulled me in for a kiss.

This time, the passion that surrounded us was palpable. I found myself running my hands over his arms, his back, and his chest. I wanted this to be real. I wanted the feelings that I felt for him to be real.

I wanted our future to be real.

I was the one who broke the kiss. I needed to keep my head straight if I was going to enter into a relationship with this man. I had more to think about than me. Blake was my priority.

Jackson didn't seem too happy when I pulled back. And when he leaned in for another kiss, I pressed my forefinger to his lips.

"We need to stop that," I whispered, my desires fighting against my words.

Jackson growled, but he must have realized that I was serious. He dropped his hands to the counter on either side of me and leaned forward, his head down. He took a few deep breaths and straightened. "Fine. But I want you to note my protest."

I laughed, enjoying the fact that he was smiling. "Duly noted."

He chuckled for a moment before he grew serious. Our gazes locked as an unspoken feeling passed between us. He liked me like I liked him. That thought caused my heart to swell.

I hadn't been crazy. That was a relief.

My gaze trailed down his face to his scar. Without

thinking, I reached out and ran my fingers down it. The tissue was tight and knotted.

Jackson didn't move. Instead, he watched me with such intensity that it took my breath away.

"What happened here?" I finally managed to ask as I moved to drop my hand.

Jackson reached out and grasped it, bringing my fingertips back to his scar. He held them there before he released them. "My stepfather used to beat my mom. One time, I got in the way to stop him." His voice was deep and gravelly. And it broke my heart.

"I'm so sorry." My voice cracked with emotion.

Jackson shrugged. "It wasn't your fault. He was an —" He shook his head as he leaned back for a moment as if to look for Blake. "A poopy head," he finished.

"A poopy head?"

Jackson turned his attention back to me. "A poopy head."

I reached out and touched his scar once more. Then I let my hand fall back to my lap. "I hope he's out of your life."

Jackson nodded. "Yeah. He left a few years before my mom passed."

I furrowed my brow. This man had such a tragic story. Every time he spoke, it got worse and worse. "I'm sorry."

His lips tipped up into a sad smile, and he shook his head. "It's okay." Then he paused. "She would have liked you."

I pressed my hand to my chest. "Me?"

He nodded. "She was a lot like you. Strong."

As much as his words made my heart sing, there was a part of me that shrunk back. He thought I was strong? I'd made so many wrong choices in my life, and all of them affected my son. He was where he was today because of my mistakes.

I was anything but strong.

"Even if you don't believe me, I see it," Jackson said as he leaned in and caught my gaze with his. There was so much warmth and affection there that I wanted to jump in with both feet and believe him, but I couldn't.

He didn't know the whole story. There was so much that we didn't know about each other. Sure, we could kiss like in an old-timey movie, but that didn't mean we could build a life together.

And I needed to be with a man that wanted forever, not just now.

"Jackson, I—"

"I'm going blind."

I stopped, the words I was going to say quickly slipping from my thoughts. "Blind?"

He pulled away and crossed to the other side of the kitchen, where he leaned against the counter and folded his arms. "Before you go into a lecture about how I'm too good for you, I thought you should know." He cleared his throat, and I could see his emotions rising up inside of him. "I'm going blind. I'm at about fifty percent vision." His voice deepened. "I'm broken."

I wasn't sure what to say. It wasn't because I was startled by his confession—even though I was. It was more that I was surprised he felt he needed to share this with me. That he trusted me enough to tell me.

"Will you go all the way blind?" I asked, and then I wanted to take my words back. Out of all the things to say, I chose to ask that?

What was wrong with me?

I shook my head before he could respond. "Never mind. Don't answer that."

His smile was small, but it made me feel better. "It's okay. I like it when you ask about my future." He pushed his hand through his hair. "It means that I might still have one."

My heart ached at his words, so I stepped forward and wrapped my hand around his forearm. He'd folded his arms across his chest, so I wiggled my fingers between them. He was so warm, and it had a healing effect on my body.

I could feel his gaze on me as he stood there. I felt as if I were melting. It was both exhilarating and terrifying at the same time.

"You do have a future," I whispered as I tipped my face toward him. The air around us grew heated as we stared at each other. I wanted to kiss him again. I wanted to feel his arms wrapped around my body. I wanted…him.

And it seemed, by the way Jackson was staring at me, he wanted the same thing.

We were moments away from kissing when a loud sound pulled us out of our trance. We both pulled back and glanced toward the door.

"Did you hear that?" Jackson asked.

I wanted to shake my head. I wanted to return to the moment we'd been in just before. I wanted to hide away in his house and pretend that the rest of the world didn't exist, but I couldn't. And from the frantic way someone was ringing the doorbell, they had no intention of leaving.

"Someone's at the door," I said with a sigh.

He looked grumpy as he stomped over and pulled it open. I didn't realize until the sun surrounded him that he was still in his swim trunks and shirt.

"Penny?" he asked, and before he could move, Maggie's mom stepped into the house.

"We need to speak."

Jackson's body stiffened as he glanced over his shoulder at me. There was a pleading in his gaze. He was worried, and suddenly, I knew about what. I was the only one who knew he was going blind. I wasn't sure what his relationship was with Penny, but he wanted me to remain quiet about it around her.

I quickly nodded my head before I moved behind the nearby cupboard. This seemed like a private conversation, and I didn't want him to feel as if I were eavesdropping.

"Where have you been? I've been waiting around to talk to you all day."

"I was out."

Penny scoffed. "Well, it's time to stop fooling around here and come back." Then she sighed. It sounded loaded with emotion. I wasn't sure what was going on, but I knew that whatever it was, it couldn't be good.

"Can we talk about this later?" Jackson asked.

I peeked around the corner to see him standing closer to her. His shoulders were tight as he hunched forward. Penny's eyes widened, and then she sighed. "How about we take this to the porch?"

Jackson glanced over his shoulder at me, and I tucked myself back into the corner where I was certain he couldn't see me. He nodded, and they both stepped out onto the porch, Jackson shutting the door behind him.

I stood there in silence for a few moments before I emerged from my hiding spot. I felt so confused. Was there something he wasn't telling me? What was his deal with Penny, and why did she keep coming around?

The man told me about his condition, but he couldn't tell me about this? Why?

I paced in the kitchen, wishing that the blinds were open, so I could at least try to read their body language. Was he mad? Were they...romantic?

I shook my head. That was a definite no. Even though Maggie's mother was beautiful, I doubted that Jackson could kiss me like that if he was romantically involved with another woman.

I touched my lips as the memory of kissing him flooded my senses. My kisses with Dave had never been like this. He was always so reserved. Held back. Dave kissed me like it was his job—not his desire.

But with Jackson, it was different. I could feel his passion for me. I could feel the want he had in his fingertips. I was what he wanted, and he let me know that. To the point where it took my breath away.

I must have lost myself in the memory of our kiss, because suddenly, the front door opened, and Jackson appeared. He looked upset as he shut the door behind him and mumbled something under his breath. I waited for him to turn around before I offered him a sympathetic smile.

"Everything okay?"

He studied me for a moment before he pushed off the door and headed across the room. "Yeah. I'm fine." He opened the fridge and took out another beer. After cracking the tab, he took a long drink.

I wondered if I should ask him what his relationship was with Penny, but then I decided to wait. I wanted Jackson to open up to me voluntarily. That made it mean more.

After he finished, he set his can down and turned to me. "We used to work together. I quit because of..." He let his voice trail off while he drew a circle in the air in front of his face. I nodded, and he continued. "She doesn't know why I quit, but that woman won't take no for an answer. It's like she's got someone hounding her to get me back."

He was talking in such vague terms that I wasn't sure

what he meant. Why wouldn't he just tell me what she wanted? "She wants you to come back to work? Where would you be 'coming back' to?"

He pushed his hands through his hair. "Doesn't matter. I'm not going back. I live here now." He kept his gaze toward the ground through our entire conversation until the last two words left his lips. Suddenly, he was staring up at me like I was all that existed in this world. "With you."

My entire body warmed at his words. Despite the fact that I wanted to know more, I allowed my curiosity to fizzle away. After all, Jackson would eventually talk to me. He would tell me what was going on, and then I could help him in the way that he needed.

But for now, I was just going to enjoy the newness of our relationship and not allow myself to get hung up on the future.

Blake woke up a few minutes later complaining of hunger. Jackson and I whipped him up some lunch, which he ate in record time. While he and Jackson played Mario Kart, I started cleaning.

I was still Jackson's housekeeper, and I still needed to be paid. Plus, I'd made a commitment. So, despite Jackson telling me to sit down and then proceeding to give me looks each time I passed by him, I chose to ignore him.

I was a woman of my word.

By six, I was tired, and Blake was getting cranky. My

phone chimed, so I slipped it from my back pocket and swiped the screen on.

Clementine: I forgot to text everyone, but there's a book club meeting at my studio tonight! I'll be handing out the books for us to read, so it should be fast.

I sent a thumbs-up and then slipped my phone back into my pocket and turned to face my demon of a child. "Come on, buddy. We should go."

Jackson sat up and set his phone on the side table next to him. He'd allowed Blake to watch a movie while he listened to an audiobook.

"You're leaving?"

My stomach leapt at his response. He wanted us to stay. And even though I wanted to stay as well, I didn't want to wear him out. Blake could be a lot, and I had my quirks as well.

"Yeah. Clementine just texted about an impromptu book club meeting, and it's Blake's witching hour." I reached down to heft my son up onto my hip. When he didn't want to do something, he went stiff.

"Oh," Jackson said.

I glanced over and reveled in the fact that he looked genuinely disappointed. "We'll be back tomorrow."

"How about I watch Blake?"

His words stopped me. I glanced over to see his earnest expression. "No. I couldn't ask you to do that." I waved off his offer. Even though it was nice that he wanted to take an active role in my son's life, I knew how

Blake could be. I didn't want to chase Jackson away just yet.

"Please? I want to help."

For a man who spent most of his time sitting in front of the TV watching sports, it was strange to see him so passionate about something. And it was even stranger that the thing he was passionate about was babysitting.

"I wanna stay with Jackson," Blake said as he pushed away from my chest in an effort to get me to put him down.

Not wanting to fight with my thirty-pound toddler, I let him slip to the floor. When his feet touched the ground, he waddled over to Jackson, who picked him up. He shrugged as he motioned to Blake. "The kid wants to stay here."

I was torn between wrestling my toddler into my car and then into my house or just giving in and allowing the two of them to hang out for the evening. That internal struggle only lasted for a moment until thoughts of sitting in the car alone and listening to my music without Blake's screams washed over me.

That made the decision easy.

I blew out my breath as I raised my finger and wiggled it at Blake. "You'll be good for Jackson?"

Blake crossed his heart with his little chubby finger. "Promise."

"We'll be fine, I swear." Jackson took a step toward me while he raised his hand to block Blake's gaze. Then he took that moment to brush his lips against mine. "I'll take good care of him. Enjoy yourself. You deserve it."

My mind was hazy as I pulled back to meet Jackson's gaze. Between the kiss and what he was saying, I was putty in his hands. Don't give me a ripped model, give me a man who kisses me and takes care of my son. *That's* the romance I want.

I felt scared, but I pushed those thoughts aside. I'd already seen Jackson with Blake. I knew that they were good together. Plus, I'd only be gone long enough to pick up the book, and then I'd head straight back.

So I planted a kiss on my son's head, grabbed my purse, and slipped on my shoes. I pulled open the front door, and before I left, I turned around to see that Jackson had set Blake down on the counter and was in the process of making macaroni and cheese. They looked like two peas in a pod.

And that's when I realized I just might be able to have this. A family. A man I loved. A father for my son.

Even though it was scary to allow myself to hope, I couldn't keep from nudging my doubt to the side.

It was possible that I could have everything I wanted.

For the first time in a long time, I felt...happy.

NINETEEN

Penny

$\mathcal{I}$ sat in my room, staring at my emails. I tried to read them, but nothing was registering. My head felt cloudy, and to be honest, I was exhausted. My conversation with Jackson had fallen flat. He wasn't interested in going back, and he'd demanded that I stop coming around. He wasn't going to change his mind no matter what I said.

It was as if no matter what I did to fix my mistakes, people weren't changing their minds. Maggie was distant. Jackson made up his mind to stay.

I felt as if I were in a sea of people, and yet no matter how much I screamed, I wasn't heard. People weren't taking notice. It was as if I didn't matter.

That was a lonely and heart-wrenching place to be.

My gaze drifted from my computer over to the small tray sitting on my nightstand. I'd asked Maggie to find me one the other day, so I could get started on the bracelet I wanted to make her. I had every intention of finishing it, but after our conversation this morning, I had lost all motivation.

I wanted to give it to her without any strings attached, but I feared the heartbreak I would feel if she didn't appreciate it as much as I hoped she would.

I'd be putting my heart out there, only to have her reject it. With everything going on in my life, I wasn't sure I would survive my daughter dismissing me.

It would crush me.

So there it sat as another reminder of my failures.

Three soft knocks pulled me out of my quick descent into madness. I glanced up and called out a soft, "Come in." I was too tired to say anything more.

"Penny?" Maggie called out as she opened the door and peeked through the opening.

I sat up straight, closing my computer and setting it on the tray with her bracelet. "Yeah." I pressed my fingers into my cheeks in hopes that I would look more alive.

Maggie pushed the door open further and glanced around as if she were nervous to come in. I wanted to invite her but then pushed that thought from my mind. If she wanted to come in, she would. The last thing she needed was a pushy mom forcing her out of her comfort zone.

"Clem wanted me to bring the books with me tonight." She shrugged.

"Oh." I pulled my comforter off my lap. "Yeah. They're in my closet. Let me get them."

Maggie held up her hand and ventured further into the room. "Stay. I'll get them."

Not sure what to do, I paused for a moment before I settled back down in my bed. I watched as Maggie opened the closet door and pulled out the box. It took her a moment to get it situated between her arms, but once she did, she gave me a soft smile.

"Thanks for this. It's really sweet that you're letting us read one of your books."

I waved away her thanks. "It's the least I can do. Hopefully, you all leave reviews." Even though Jackson still refused to publish, I wasn't ready to give up on him just yet.

Maggie nodded. "I'll let the girls know."

Silence fell as we both nodded. I hated seeing my daughter look so uncomfortable. I hated even more that I'd been the one to make her feel that way. Magnolia was her safe place, and I had to go and ruin it by suggesting that I move here.

It had been selfish of me to assume that she would be happy at that proposition. I was here to help my daughter, and I was failing at that.

I needed to remedy my mistake.

"I'll be leaving in the morning," I blurted out. Then I pinched my lips together. What was I thinking? Why tomorrow? I wanted to do the right thing, but I was dying inside. Apparently, my subconscious fear was stronger than I'd thought.

"Tomorrow? Really?"

I nodded. There was no going back now. "Yeah, I'm needed at work. But I'll be here for the wedding," I hurried to add.

She was quiet, and I wished that I could read her thoughts. Her expression was soft, and I couldn't tell if she was sad or relieved. I felt like a fool to think she would ever be sad about me leaving.

"Oh. Well, I understand," she said as she shifted the box.

Realizing that she was standing there with a heavy box pressing into her arms, I motioned toward the door. "I'll say goodbye before I leave tomorrow."

Her gaze shifted from the door to me. She nodded a few times before she said, "That would be nice."

I smiled, forcing my strength to the surface. Maggie was better without me. I needed to keep chanting that in my mind. Maggie was better off, Sampson and Scotts was better off, even Jackson was better off.

I was beginning to wonder who actually needed me. These last few weeks had taught me there was no one who wanted me around.

That was a dark place to be.

Not wanting to delve deeper into my thoughts, I grabbed a nearby book and flipped it open. "Have fun at your book club," I said as I turned a page, praying that

Maggie would take me seriously and think that I was reading.

From the corner of my eye, I saw her study me for a moment before she sighed. I could tell that she had more she wanted to say, and I prayed that she would keep it to herself.

I wasn't ready for the conversation where she told me everything I'd done wrong. And how our relationship issues were my fault. She would be correct. Our issues did stem from me. But I wasn't in the headspace to process the emotions that would come from her words.

I needed time to understand why I felt the way I did. Entering into an emotionally charged conversation with my daughter wasn't going to help me figure out where I was at. So I held my breath as I waited for her to leave.

Thankfully, she didn't speak. She just turned and slipped out of my room, the sound of the closed door echoing behind her. I let out the breath I'd been holding as silence engulfed me.

I was once again alone.

That was where I was comfortable. When I was alone, no one could hurt me. When I was alone, I was in control. I only had to worry about myself. No one could hurt me, and even better, I couldn't hurt anyone else.

I set the book I'd been pretending to read down next to me and snuggled deeper under my comforter. My emotions were a mess, and I was too exhausted to think. I just wanted to lie here and disappear. Disappear back into my world. Create a safe space around me where I didn't have to face my past or those that I'd hurt.

How does one fix the problems they created? What did Maggie need to be happy again?

It seemed like ever since I came back into the picture, things for my daughter had gotten worse. She was sadder, and I hated that. I didn't want her to feel this way. Especially not when she was planning her wedding.

Tears pricked my eyes as realization passed over me. I was the source of my daughter's pain, and if I wanted her to be happy, I knew what I needed to do. I needed to walk away. I needed to remove myself from the situation and allow her to be the one thing she would never be with me around…happy.

I draped my arm over my eyes as I took in some deep breaths. I hadn't felt this hopeless and unhappy in a long time. It was as if I were facing the demons that I'd kept at bay for so long.

Why had I thought that coming here to fix my relationship with Maggie would somehow be beneficial for me? I felt alone. Nothing had been fixed, and the only thing I'd accomplished was to destroy the dam inside of me that kept these feelings contained. Now, I was facing them, and it was ugly.

I was going to leave Magnolia more broken than I'd been when I got here. My entire body felt numb as I pulled my arm down and stared up at the ceiling. The blank canvas seemed to help me process my thoughts.

Like I was staring at an empty page where I could write my feelings.

Where did I go from here? I blinked as those words formed above me.

I hated how confused I felt. Right now, I wasn't sure who I was or what my future held, and that uncertainty was stifling. Like a weight around my shoulders pulling me down.

I wanted to pull the weight off. I wanted relief, but it wasn't going to happen.

Not for me.

I was going to be alone forever. It was time I started accepting that. It was time I moved on from trying to convince my daughter to let me into her life. She was happier without me, and I needed to let her be that way.

If I loved my daughter, I would leave. I would take away the stress she felt while being around me.

I'd spent my whole life sacrificing my daughter's happiness for my own, and I was going to put a stop to that. I sat up on the bed and pulled the tray with her unfinished bracelet onto my lap.

For the first time, I'd finish something for her. I would put her wants ahead of my own. And then I would leave.

For good.

TWENTY

Fiona

I pulled open the door to Clementine's studio and let it shut behind me. The bells that hung from the inside door handle jingled to announce my arrival. The chatter coming from the back stopped, and a moment later, Clem appeared with a huge smile on her face.

"Fiona! We were waiting for you," she said as she crossed the room and pulled me into a hug.

It felt good being here. I'd left Blake with Jackson, and I was ready for some girl time and advice. My head was still swimming from my kiss with Jackson and the potential of our relationship becoming something real. I needed a place where I could sift through what had happened and come to a healthy conclusion.

These were just the women to help me do it.

"Come on back."

I nodded as I followed her to the studio that Jake had

set up. Clementine had been serious when she talked about offering pole dancing lessons. To make sure people felt safe, she had walled off a small space in the back to keep any onlookers from seeing in.

Even though I hadn't signed up yet, if and when I did, I certainly didn't want half of Magnolia to see how awful I was at it. Give me some time to learn before you give me an audience.

Maggie and Shari were sitting on the mats, dipping bread into warm cheese, while Victoria was on her phone in the corner. It was funny that our book club that had started out with so many women had distilled down to the five of us. I wasn't going to complain, I liked that we were small in numbers. It made the book club feel more intimate. And when you're talking about your issues, the fewer people who knew, the better.

"Glass of wine?" Clem asked as she headed over to the small table against the far wall. There were a few bottles resting on it.

"Red, please," I said as I dropped my purse next to my shoes at the door. Then I padded over to Maggie and Shari and sat down next to them.

Maggie was mid-chew, so Shari greeted me. "How's Blake?"

I'd just dipped some bread into the fondue, so I ate it quickly before I responded. "He's good."

"Your mom has him?"

My cheeks heated, and I cursed them for giving me away. Realizing that I wasn't going to be able to evade

Shari's curiosity, I decided to be upfront. Even though I wasn't quite ready to talk about Jackson, I knew we would discuss it eventually. Might as well start now.

"He's with Jackson."

Maggie perked up. I hadn't realized how sad she looked...until I talked about Jackson. "Jackson Richards?"

I nodded. "The guy that your mom works with."

"Wait, Blake is with some strange man that works with Penny?" Shari looked perturbed as she glanced between Maggie and me.

"Yeah. I'm working for him as his housekeeper." The memory of him pressing me against the counter in the kitchen flooded my mind, and my cheeks felt like they were on fire. If my blush hadn't given me away earlier, I was fairly certain a satellite could spot me now.

"What does that mean?" Shari narrowed her eyes as she leaned closer to me.

I feigned innocence. "What?"

She wiggled her forefinger in my direction. "Your face is really red." Then her eyes widened. "Did something happen?"

I pressed the back of my hands to my cheeks and pulled back. "I'm not saying."

"It did!" Shari was screeching now.

Maggie looked confused, and Victoria turned to shoot Shari a dirty look. If Shari saw, she didn't try to calm down. I guess that was a perk of dating the brother of the woman currently giving you a death stare—you stopped caring what they think.

I shushed Shari before she woke up the whole town. Thankfully, Clementine had returned with our drinks. I savored my drink, which allowed me to take a moment to think before I responded. How much was I going to tell them?

Did Jackson want them to know what had transpired between us?

I doubted it.

"We're just good friends," I muttered after I ate another piece of cheese-coated bread.

Shari rested her hands behind her as she leaned back. "Uh-huh. I don't believe you. A person doesn't blush that hard for a *good friend*."

I narrowed my eyes at her. She was not making this easy.

"What is going on that you had to yell that loud?" Victoria said. She'd tucked her phone away in her pocket and sat down next to me. She glanced between me and Shari as she reached forward to grab a piece of bread.

"Fiona is having a fling with the brooding recluse," Shari offered, wiggling her eyebrows in my direction as she spoke.

"It's not a fling," I muttered.

Before I realized what I'd said, Shari squealed. "So it is something!"

I loved Shari like a sister, but I was seconds away from slugging her in the shoulder. I was having a hard enough time trying to convince myself that my kiss with Jackson hadn't meant anything, and here she was, pumping up my adrenaline and getting me to hope that it meant something more than it did.

I needed to remain calm about this, and she wasn't helping me.

"Spill," Clementine said as she bumped my shoulder with hers.

I took a deep breath. I was going to need to give her something, or these women were not going to let me leave tonight. "He kissed me."

From the round-as-saucers eyes that peered back at me, I realized very quickly that I'd made a mistake. I wanted to take it back and only allude to what had happened, but unfortunately, that ship had sailed.

I'd said the words, and now I needed to deal with the fallout.

"Tell us everything," Maggie said as she leaned in.

It was strange, having their undivided attention. I wasn't used to it, but I was also excited to navigate the situation I now found myself in. So I took in a deep breath and started.

It was fun to watch their expressions as I went through the hills and valleys of what had happened between us. When I got to the kiss, they all gasped—well, minus Victoria, but she wasn't one who was shocked easily. When I finished, they all looked at each other as they settled back on the floor. They had been inching closer to me throughout the whole story.

"Wow," Shari said. I was learning that, despite her being cheated on, she was the most romantic at heart. I think it was Danny. He had definitely encouraged her acceptance of romance back into her life. It was fun to watch.

"Yeah," I said, the word landing heavy in the air.

"So what are you going to do?" Clem asked.

I shrugged. "I don't know. I mean, I like him, but I feel like he has so many secrets. And I'm not sure if I'm in a place in my life to try to uncover them."

"Take your time, then. I mean, if he's not ready to be completely honest and open himself up to you, then you should keep your distance." We all turned to Maggie. There was a crack in her voice as if she knew exactly what I was going through.

"Everything okay, Mags?" Clementine asked.

Maggie's expression fell as she brought her knees to her chest and hugged them. I could see the tears that were threatening to fall. "It's just my mom. I thought things were going well between us, but she's leaving tomorrow." A tear slipped down her cheek, and she angrily wiped it away. "I tried so hard to include her in my wedding. I invited her to everything—against Archer's wishes. And now she's leaving. And I don't know what I did wrong." She sniffled and wiped her cheeks on her knees.

My heart ached for her. I knew what it was like to struggle with your relationship with your mom, and I knew how much Maggie wanted to have a better relationship with her mother. It's hard when you try, and the other person doesn't give.

"I'm sorry, Maggie," Shari said as she wrapped her arm around Maggie's shoulders.

Maggie was quiet. We sat with her, waiting for her to break the silence. A few seconds passed before she nodded and straightened. "I'm sorry, guys. I'm totally bringing down the group. We were excited for Fiona, and now I've made everyone depressed."

We all shook our heads in unison.

"It's totally fine. I get it," I said as I offered her a small smile. "We've all struggled. That's what we are here for."

She smiled at me. "Thanks." Then she furrowed her brow. "Is Jackson going with Penny?"

I shrugged. "Maybe. I'm not sure. He hasn't really talked to me about his job."

Maggie furrowed her brow. "He hasn't told you that he's an author?"

I blinked and then slowly shook my head. "No. He hasn't."

Maggie looked as confused as I felt. I could tell that she was trying to figure out what was going on, but then she just shrugged. "Strange. He has a book that Penny's publishing house is putting out, but he's pulled it for some reason." She grabbed a chunk of bread and dipped it. "Seems like he has a lot of secrets, like you said."

It was all making sense now. He was going blind. He was an author. He was a *famous* author. I couldn't imagine the pressure he was under, and to add his disease on top of it—that couldn't be easy.

My heart ached for him.

But then something Maggie said wiggled its way into my mind. Now that Penny was leaving...was Jackson? Had they worked things out? I hadn't heard the rest of their conversation, could Jackson have agreed to return?

Had I just put my heart into the hands of the wrong man again?

I felt so confused. I'd come here for answers, and I was going to leave with more doubt than I walked in with. Why had Jackson been so reserved with me? Why couldn't he just say what was going on with him?

Anger and confusion began to bubble up inside of me. My agitation was making me antsy, so I stood and walked over to the beverage table and poured some more wine in my cup. I couldn't have much more since I was driving, but I needed to look like I was doing something.

The girls returned their attention to Maggie, who was giving them details about the wedding. In all honesty, I was grateful that they'd changed topics. I wasn't ready for any more revelations about Jackson, and I didn't want them to tell me that everything was going to be alright. I'd already been here once.

I'd already fallen for a man who wasn't the person I'd thought he was.

Just as I felt myself spiral, my phone rang. Grateful for the distraction, I pulled it from my pocket and glanced down.

Jackson.

My heart began to pound. This wasn't good. If this was my reaction from just seeing his name, what was I going to do when I went there to pick up Blake?

I finally answered after the fifth ring. It was drawing the attention of the others in the room, so I decided it was time to take the call before they asked who it was. "Hello?"

"Fiona?"

He sounded frantic. Why was he frantic?

"Yeah. Is everything okay? Is Blake okay?" My heart was hammering in my chest now. Not from confusion but worry.

"I'm sorry," he whispered.

My whole body went numb. "What happened?"

"I lost Blake. I can't find him."

The time it took for me to register what Jackson had said, tell the girls at the book club, and get in the car and drive over to his house passed over me. It was like it was a blur and slow-motion at the same time. Maggie insisted that she drive, and the other girls climbed into the car before I could tell them no.

By the time we pulled up in Jackson's driveway, I felt completely overwhelmed. I wanted to jump out, but I was pinned between Clementine and Victoria. And even though they were moving to get out, it felt as if they were purposely going slow.

Thankfully, I held it together, and as soon as my feet were on the ground, I sprinted to the house. Colten was standing in the doorway, talking to Jackson. When his gaze met mine, his face paled.

"Where is he?" I asked as I pushed past Colten and barreled into Jackson's house.

"He's fine. We found him ten minutes ago. He's inside eating a yogurt," Colten said. He followed after me while Jackson moved to the side.

I glanced at him for a moment before I scanned the room for Blake. He was snuggled up in a blanket with a spoon and a container. He was happily spooning yogurt into his mouth—and managing to plop a few globs on the blanket in the process.

"He's okay?" I asked as I crossed the room and knelt down in front of him. I ran my hand over his head and face just to make sure he wasn't bleeding somewhere that I couldn't see.

He complained and moved to the side. "Stop, Mommy," he said as he returned to watching his show.

My entire body was shaking now. I stood and made my way back to Colten, who was talking to the girls.

"Where did you find him?" I asked, my gaze slipping over to Jackson, who had disappeared into the shadows. I wanted to scream. I wanted to cry. But I couldn't find it in me to do anything but stare at Colten as he spoke.

Apparently, Blake had slipped out of the house while Jackson went to the bathroom. He wandered down the beach until Scarlett found him and called Colten. Jackson had searched but didn't know which direction he went and ended up going the opposite way.

Thankfully, he'd stayed out of the water. Besides being a bit cold and a tad shook up, he was my perfect little boy.

"You're sure he's fine?" I asked again. Even though Colten had already assured me that everything was fine, I needed to hear those words one more time.

"He's fine. I had Brittney over here, and she checked him out. She gave him a clean bill of health."

Brittney was the island's PA who had just taken over for Dr. Willis when he retired. She'd moved here a few months ago, and I'd heard Maggie talk about inviting her to join our book club. I wanted to tell Colten that Blake needed to see a real doctor. Someone who didn't just get her medical license last year, but I bit my tongue.

I could tell that Blake was fine, and there was no need to be rude.

"Okay," I whispered.

It was a strange sensation, going from complete panic to relief. It was as if the muscles that had been keeping my body running all decided to relax at once. I felt myself begin to drop, and a moment later, a set of arms wrapped around me, holding me up.

"Th-thanks," I stammered as I glanced over to see Jackson standing next to me.

His jaw was tense, and his gaze was focused forward. I wanted to wiggle away from him. After this experience, I wasn't really in the mood to talk to him or be touched by him.

If Jackson sensed my hesitation, he didn't do

anything about it. Instead, he bent down, hooked his arm under my knees, and pulled me up to his chest. My wretched heart began to pound. I felt so safe and secure in his arms—and I hated it.

He was leaving. I could feel him pulling away from me. Even though him losing Blake had been an honest mistake—if I were honest with myself, I'd done the same thing on numerous occasions—it didn't change the fact that he hadn't spoken to me since I got here.

All I'd got from him was a stony look and a bad attitude.

My emotions were so muddled, and I felt completely confused by everything.

Jackson set me down on the couch. He never once made eye contact with me. I collapsed into the cushions, the desire to relax winning over the desire to fight back.

Shari sat next to me, and I appreciated her calming spirit. I was grateful for my friends in this moment. They seemed to know what I needed and were willing to step up and be what I couldn't be for myself.

Clementine and Maggie ushered the deputies from the house while Victoria gave a statement to Colten. Eventually, everything wound down, and it was just me, Shari, Blake, and Jackson left in the house.

I sighed as I closed my eyes and tipped my head back. I was frustrated that Jackson hadn't said anything to me since I got here. I had so many questions, and I wasn't getting any answers.

I was a volcano waiting to erupt.

"I'll take Blake home and wait for you," Shari said as she moved to stand.

I reached out and grabbed her hand. She hesitated before giving me a big smile. "You need to talk to him."

My gaze drifted over to Jackson, and realization hit me. She was right. As much as I didn't want to, I needed to talk to him.

So I nodded, and she stood. Blake was all too eager to go with Shari. He jumped into her arms and hugged her tight as she carried him from the house. Even though she shut the door quietly, with the stillness in the air, it was as if she slammed it.

The sound of the door latching echoed off the walls. Suddenly, we were very alone. I peeked over at Jackson to see him leaning against the far wall. That man had a way of finding all the shadows in the room. His gaze was downturned, and I took a moment to study him.

Now that my nerves had calmed, and I could finally breathe, regret settled in my chest. He felt bad about losing Blake. I knew that guilt all too well.

Once a mistake is made, it's impossible to take it back. And when that mistake involves a child, the weight of it is even heavier.

I didn't want Jackson to feel that way.

Ever.

"He's fine," I said as I slowly set my feet on the floor and stood.

Jackson didn't respond. But he must have noticed I

had moved because his entire body tensed. His jaw tightened, and his hands fisted.

"Jackson," I said softly as I stepped closer to him. When I was near, I raised my hand to touch his arm. I needed to reach him. I needed to pull him back to me before it was too late.

I was a moment away from touching him when he suddenly pulled back.

"Don't." His voice was raspy and desperate. "Don't pretend like this was okay." He stepped back.

"You made a mistake. We all do." He couldn't do this to me. Sure, I'd lost my mind when I got here, but it was my son. He couldn't blame me for that. I was telling him that I'd moved on. Blake was safe, and that was all that mattered. He didn't need to push me away.

Not when he'd given me so much hope earlier.

"We need to stop." He pushed his hair away from his face, and with that swift movement, he was staring at me. "I can't risk your safety, and I definitely can't risk Blake's." His blue eyes were once again icy.

"But—"

"I mean it. I'm going back to New York with Penny. You need to forget about me and everything I've said."

I couldn't lose him. I needed him to stop talking. I needed to convince him to stay, and I wasn't going to be able to do that if he'd already made up his mind. "Jackson, you don't mean that." My voice broke. I'd allowed this man into my life, and he was walking away? He couldn't do this to me. Not when he'd gotten me to hope that there was something real between us.

My fingers brushed his forearm, and he snapped it back like he'd been burned. His entire expression hardened, and I knew it was over. We were over.

I wasn't going to be able to convince him otherwise, and I wasn't in a place to try.

I was broken already. If I stuck around, he was going to pulverize what was left.

"Fine," I managed out. Thankfully, a crappy relationship with Dave had taught me to be strong even when I felt weak. I had the great ability to pretend like I didn't give a heck—even if that was far from the truth. "I'll send you the final invoice."

I didn't wait for him to respond. Instead, I turned on my heel, grabbed my purse, and left.

The front door slammed behind me, and once I was sure he couldn't see me, I released the breath I'd been holding. Tears slid down my cheeks as I rounded the house. I had no idea how I was going to get home, but I knew I couldn't stay here.

Just as my feet hit the gravel driveway, a voice caused me to lift my gaze. At first, I thought it was Jackson telling me to come back. My heart raced at the thought that he would pull me into his arms and never let me go.

But when my gaze landed on Colten and the sheriff car, my entire body went numb.

"Need a ride?" he asked, moving to open the passenger door.

I sniffled and nodded. Once I was inside, he shut the door, and I buckled up. He climbed into the driver's seat and started the engine. Before we took off, I turned to face him.

"I don't want to talk about Jackson." I knew they were friends, and the last thing I needed was for Colten to tell me that he really was a good guy. Right now, I needed to hate him.

"Roger that," he said softly.

The ride home was quiet, and when I got into the apartment, Blake was asleep. Mom poured me a glass of wine and sent me off to the bubble bath she'd drawn for me. From the expression on her face, I knew that Shari had filled her in on the details.

Which I was grateful for. I didn't have the energy to speak.

By the time I crawled into bed, my entire body felt weighed down by sand. My fingers, my toes, even my eyelids felt as if they weighed a hundred pounds.

I was ready to sink into sleep. What had started out as a perfect day had quickly changed. I'd been so hopeful, but now I knew that hope was futile.

I was going to be alone. I might as well start accepting that.

Jackson was out of my life, and I was certain there was no way my heart could heal from this many blows.

Love just wasn't in my future.

TWENTY-ONE

Penny

$\mathcal{I}$ don't know what I was thinking. For some reason, I'd figured that my life would return to normal once I was back in New York.

When Jackson called and told me that he was coming back with me for this book release, I celebrated. I'd come here to save my job, and I'd done just that. I wanted to ask what made him change his mind, but when I got there to pick him up the next day, he looked as if he was moments away from slugging someone—so I decided to leave it at that.

It didn't really matter. He was saving my career, and that was all that mattered. We'd never really had a close relationship, and I couldn't justify us starting now.

We were professionals, and I was ready to get back to only associating with people on that level. It kept things less messy.

But as I sat at the vanity in my apartment, a pain that

I'd never experienced before settled in my chest. I'd just gotten out of the shower, and I was in the process of getting ready for a book party for Jackson. Sampson and Scotts had moved quickly after Jackson got back and moved up the book launch. They were concerned he was going to walk again.

I pressed my hand to the left side of my ribs and took in a deep breath.

Was I having a heart attack?

I stilled my body and tried to focus on where that pain was coming from. My heartbeat felt strong, so that must be fine. Why did I feel as if an elephant was sitting on my chest?

It must just be nerves for the party. After all, I'd been back for a week already. If it was guilt for leaving Maggie and rejecting Georgette, why did it suddenly start now?

"It's just nerves," I whispered as I finished brushing blush onto my cheeks.

I dressed in a black chiffon dress, heels, and a glittery gold shawl. With my hair pulled up halfway and soft ringlets falling around my face, I smiled.

Penny Brown was back.

It felt great…sort of. For a moment, I wondered what Maggie was doing and how the wedding plans were going. She texted me a few times after I left to give me updates—which I was grateful for—but it just left me feeling hollow.

They were moving up the wedding and had decided to do it on the beach. She hoped that I could come for the ceremony but understood that I was busy. She didn't want to push me.

That just piled guilt on me. She should be mad. She should never want to speak to me again.

She should scream and yell at me and tell me what a horrible mother I was. She shouldn't ask me to come to her wedding.

And she certainly shouldn't forgive me.

I didn't deserve it.

The pain remained the entire limo ride over to Jackson's hotel. He was determined that this was his last book. Once this was over, he was out of here.

I knew I should try to convince him to stay, but I didn't have the energy. Not when I was barely able to convince myself to stay.

Sure, Burt and Kyle were happy that I got Jackson back. Tensions around the office had lessened, but I knew that wasn't forever. At some point, they were going to grow tired of me again, and then where would I be?

Right back where I was a few weeks ago.

If I'd learned anything from this debacle, it was that, in their eyes, I was disposable. They were going to use me while I was useful and then discard me when they were done.

It was up to me to decide how long I would stick around and wait.

Thankfully, Jackson was dressed and waiting at the curb when the limo pulled up. His gaze roamed over the monstrosity, and his expression morphed into one of disgust. I told Burt not to do this, but he insisted. This was going to be a show, and we needed to play along.

I knew this was the last thing that Jackson wanted. On the drive back to New York, he'd told me about his condition. At first, I was shocked, but when I parted my lips to tell him that it didn't matter, he held up his hand. He didn't want to be a charity case, and he didn't want my sympathy.

He was going to deal with it the best way he knew how—which apparently meant shutting everyone out and running.

I wanted to tell him that reacting that way only got you so far. I had enough experience with running to last both of our lifetimes; but who was I to speak?

Jackson and I were more similar than I'd known.

"Geez, why not a blimp?" he asked when he opened the back door and slipped onto the seat next to me. His shoulders were slumped, and as soon as he closed his door, the driver took off.

"I know, but Burt wanted it."

Jackson didn't respond. He leaned his head back on the seat and closed his eyes. I wanted to ask if he was exhausted or if his condition hurt his eyes, but then I decided against it. We weren't really the *share-our-feelings type*, and I didn't see that changing anytime soon.

So I turned my gaze outside of the car.

"How's being back been?" The question was out before I could stop myself. I knew Jackson didn't want to talk to me. From what I could gather, something had happened between him and Fiona, but Jackson hadn't told me anything more.

He grunted.

Which was what I expected. "Yeah. I'm the same. I keep wondering when my life will get back to normal." My voice drifted off as my gaze focused on the buildings passing by. I was no longer talking to Jackson, but myself.

"Why do I want it to go back to normal?" The question came out as a whisper. It was so strange to even utter it. It felt as if it were stuck inside of me, refusing to come out. But now that it was out in the open, I couldn't take it back. I had to face it.

"What?"

I glanced over to see that Jackson had straightened. His expression was one of annoyance and intrigue. I shook my head as I focused back outside.

"I'm just having an existential crisis."

Which was true. Everything I thought I wanted. Everything that I had worked so hard to get meant nothing without my daughter. All of these parties, all of the money, all of the accolades felt hollow and empty.

I wanted a life outside of work. I wanted a family. I wanted people in my corner who I didn't have to worry about stabbing me in the back. Harper was seconds away from taking my job—I could feel it. Burt and Kyle wouldn't bat an eye if they needed to fire me.

I was expendable to these people, and I was sick of it.

I wanted a new life. I wanted one with my daughter front and center.

"I'm done," I whispered.

"What?"

I turned to Jackson, who looked completely confused by my one-sided conversation. "I'm done," I said louder this time. I reached up and unclipped my hair. I shook it out.

Jackson looked uncomfortable. "What are you done with?"

I removed a tissue from my purse and wiped off my makeup. "This. All of this." I waved my hand to the city. The place I'd once loved. The place I'd figured I would spend the rest of my life in.

Now, it felt too busy. Too crowded. Too...much. I wanted Magnolia. I wanted the slow-paced, everyone-knows-everyone feeling. I wanted my small newspaper where I would report on Mrs. Glasgow and the new flowers in her front yard.

I wanted to get back to the life I'd lived before I threw everything away to come here.

I was done running away. It left me alone and hollow.

I was ready to live.

"We're not going to the party?" Jackson asked. He looked more alive than I'd ever seen him as he straightened up in his seat.

I shook my head. "I'm not going. You can go if you want." I pulled out my phone and opened the text chain with Burt and typed in two words. Those two little words that held the key to my happiness.

I quit.

Then I turned it on silent and slipped my phone back into my purse. I didn't need to know if they responded because it didn't matter. Nothing was going to change my mind.

"So, does that mean you're not publishing my book?"

I shrugged. "Not my problem anymore." I rolled down my window and stuck my hand out. The wind rushed over my skin, and for the first time, I felt weightless.

"Huh."

When he didn't say more, I peeked over at him. He looked unhappy. Whatever had transpired between Jackson and Fiona had left a blight on his joy. My heart went out to him. I knew what it was like to pull yourself away. To force unhappiness on yourself because you thought it would fix someone else's life.

I was beginning to learn that was a lie. A lie we tell to protect ourselves.

"Tell her," I said as I leaned over.

Jackson startled and turned to look at me. "Tell who?"

"Fiona."

His jaw tightened. "She doesn't want to have anything to do with me."

I clicked my tongue. "That's a lie."

He growled. "No it's not."

"Did you ask her?"

Silence.

"You didn't. You assume you know what's right for

her." I sighed. "I was the same. And you know what? People are pretty good at knowing what they want. What they need. If Fiona wants you, then love her enough to let her in."

He folded his arms across his chest. His demeanor was softening, which gave me hope. I was getting somewhere with him.

"I'm broken."

"We're all broken. The question is, will we allow ourselves to be put back together again." I gave him an encouraging smile. "You have to believe that you are worthy of being fixed, and then let Fiona do the rest."

He stared at me. I could see so much fear and nervousness in his gaze. I wanted to reach out and let him know that I was there—but that felt like an overstep in our relationship. So I decided to remain encouraging from a distance.

The limo slowed as it pulled in front of the hotel hosting our launch. I stared at Jackson, waiting to see what he would do. He paused, his fingers resting on the door handle.

Just when I thought he was going to give it a good tug and step out, he sighed and shook his head.

"Driver?" His voice had changed. It was stronger and more assured.

The man looked into the rearview mirror. "Yeah?"

"Drive us home."

TWENTY-TWO

Fiona

_____

$\mathcal{M}$y palms were sweating.

I rubbed my hands on my pencil skirt and glanced around the courtroom. Even though Austin assured me that this was an open-and-shut child support case, the butterflies in my stomach wouldn't calm down.

Instead, they were assaulting my insides like they were trying to break free.

"You'll be fine," Mom said as her hand appeared in my line of sight. She patted my knee a few times before returning her hand to her lap.

I knew she was trying to be supportive—but it wasn't working. The fact that she had to show me support meant I was struggling. She knew it. I knew it. And I was pretty sure that the judge was going to know it in a few minutes.

It didn't help that every part of my body hurt right now. My heart. My stomach. My head. Ever since Jackson left, I'd been a mess. It made me regret agreeing to the earlier court date.

Sitting here now, I wish I had said no.

I needed more time to prepare. I needed more time to heal. I needed more time to force myself to forget Jackson and be content with my life. With the thoughts that were swimming around in my head, I feared I would stand up to speak and word-vomit in front of the judge.

I would say everything that I was feeling, and none of it would help me.

"It'll be fine. You're a good mom, and Dave should be paying his fair share," Austin whispered as he leaned closer to me.

I took in a breath, trying to internalize his words. I guess I hoped that if I repeated them enough in my mind, I would believe them.

It wasn't working.

All I could think about was how I was now jobless. Blake was confused about what had happened to Jackson. Mom was still struggling with her finances. My big plan to fix all of our problems had imploded on me.

Now, I was about to stand up in front of a judge to explain to him why Dave needed to pay to support our son and how I was a functioning mother.

All of those words felt like a lie.

The couple in front of us were wrapping up, and my stomach flipped. We were next. I was next.

I swallowed; my mouth felt like sandpaper.

Suddenly, a bottle of water appeared next to me. I startled and turned to see Shari standing behind me. Clementine, and Victoria were lined up beside her. Their smiles were big—well, not Victoria's, but the small one she had was an improvement over her perpetually pinched lips—and their gazes were ones of encouragement.

I took the water bottle and mouthed a quick *thank-you*. Before we could talk further, Austin nudged me. It was my turn.

The entire talk with the judge felt like a blur. Thankfully, Austin knew what he was doing and helped coach me along. My body felt numb as I stood there, answering questions. It didn't help that Dave was standing just a few feet away from me. His presence had me all discombobulated.

The hearing didn't last too long, and the judge ruled in my favor. Dave was to pay child support starting next month, which included a percentage of back pay. I wanted to cheer, but I couldn't. I hated the fact that I'd had to bring him to court to get him to help his son.

Even now that this was finished, it didn't mean my life was going to be easier. Things were still hard for me and were going to continue being hard. Without a job and with Mom struggling to pay back her loans, this was a tiny shovel for a big hole.

Once we were excused, I tried to catch Dave's eye before he walked out. But he didn't seem interested in speaking to me. He walked right past me and out the door.

There wasn't a lot I wanted to say to him, but I wanted to make sure things were going to be okay between us. After all, we both had a son to raise. Blake wasn't going to have a father in his life if Dave insisted on acting like this.

Sure, I wanted my ex to pay his fair share, but that didn't mean that Dave had to take his anger out on Blake. We could find a way to coexist peacefully.

We could.

But Dave didn't seem to feel that way, and in a moment, he was gone.

I blew out my breath as I made my way out of the courtroom and into the foyer. Austin and Shari were talking. The other gals were milling around. I wasn't sure what they were waiting for. I hoped it wasn't me.

I loved my friends, but with the way I was feeling right now, I needed some air. I needed some space. I needed to breathe.

"I'll be right back," I whispered as I sidestepped the ladies and zeroed in on the exit. I winced, hoping that they wouldn't ask to follow.

Thankfully, they either picked up on my need to be alone or didn't hear me—because a moment later, I was outside in the bright sun, and no one had followed after me.

The door swung closed, and I moved to lean against

the building. I took in a deep breath as I tipped my face toward the sky and allowed the sun's rays to wash over me. I closed my eyes and stilled my mind.

The truth was, I was so out of sorts because of my heart. It was hemorrhaging right now. The memory of the night Jackson left kept playing over and over in my mind. I wanted to forget him. I wanted to pretend that everything was okay...but I couldn't.

Not when I was as broken as I was.

The sound of someone clearing their throat forced me back into the present. I wiped at the tears that had slipped down my cheeks. I felt like an idiot for crying and even more so for interrupting someone's smoke break with my mental breakdown.

"I'm sorry," I whispered as I turned to face the stranger I'd just barged in on.

My entire body froze as I stared at a pair of very familiar dark glasses. I blinked a few times, cursing myself for seeing Jackson everywhere I went. Just because this person had sunglasses like his, that didn't make him Jackson.

I kept my gaze down as I moved to step past him. Since I'd exited a side door, it was locked on the outside. If I was going to return to my friends, I needed to go back through the front entrance.

But the stranger who wore the same glasses as Jackson stepped in front of me.

"Fiona."

Now I was hearing things. How did he know my name? And why did he sound like Jackson?

My entire body went numb as understanding began to register in my mind.

It wasn't some figment of my imagination. He sounded and looked like Jackson because...it *was* Jackson.

I froze. He was standing there with his dark hair falling over his forehead and his hands shoved deep into his pockets. His stance was so unsure that it made my heart pound. I was used to his gruff demeanor. If he looked worried, that meant he was doing something he didn't know how to do.

"Wha-what are you doing here?" My cheeks heated as I scrambled to gain control of my thoughts. Jackson was here. We were talking. I needed to focus, so I didn't come across as some heartbroken, bumbling idiot.

He studied me for a moment before turning his attention outward. "I, uh..." He cleared his throat. His voice lingering in the air around us. My body was tense as I waited for him to continue. "I was worried you would feel alone."

I had not been expecting that. My brain felt frozen as I digested his words. "You were worried about me?" Hot tears stung my eyelids. I hated that he was here. I hated that he came back. And I hated that he'd made his way back to Magnolia because he was concerned for me.

He looked at me. Then he slowly nodded.

That was all I needed for the dam to break. Tears flowed down my cheeks. I wanted to scream at him. I wanted to curse him. I wanted to hate him…but I didn't.

Seeing him here. Having him come back to support me during a time that was hard, it made me love him even more. My stupid heart hadn't learned any lessons. Instead, it decided the best thing to do was to throw all logic out the window and just feel.

Dumb heart.

I'd been led astray by it before, and I was determined to change my ways. So despite the fact that all I wanted to do was run into his arms and feel his heart beat against his chest—I wasn't going to do that. My head was going to guide me from now on.

The silence that settled around us was deafening. I wanted him to speak and stay silent at the same time. I took in a deep breath, thankful that my tears had subsided.

"Well, I'm fine. So you can go back to New York and live your fancy author life." I winced at the wavering in my voice. I didn't want him to leave. I was screaming inside for him to apologize, so we could start over.

I wanted him in my life, but if he didn't want the same—I wanted him to leave.

"I'm not."

I paused, his two-word sentence running over me. "You're not what?"

He cleared his throat again and pushed his hair from

his face. "I'm not okay with leaving again. I'm not fine. I don't want to live in New York."

My heart began to pound. I wanted to call it out for its traitorous reaction. I was supposed to remain strong, and here I was, ready to run into his arms if he asked me.

How was I ever going to get over Jackson if I kept imagining he was asking for things that he wasn't asking for?

"So what *do* you want? Is that why you came here? Do you want me to tell you what to do?" I felt angry and frustrated and lonely. It was a strange sensation to have all of those emotions crashing into one another.

"I want you."

The world around me stopped moving. His words lingered in the air, and for a moment, I almost allowed myself to believe he'd said them. Then I shook my head. That was ridiculous. I was ridiculous.

But before I could figure out what to say, he was approaching me. There was some hesitation in his gait, but he was moving toward me. My entire body tensed.

"I'm so sorry, Fiona. I know I don't deserve you, and I definitely don't deserve Blake. I shouldn't have lost him that night, and I can't stop thinking about what might have happened to him if Scarlett hadn't found him." His voice broke, and even though I couldn't see his eyes, I could see his struggle in his body language and expression.

He was hurting inside, and that hurt me too.

I needed to know where he was going with this before I responded. I needed to know if he was just here to break my heart again or if he wanted something more. "We all make mistakes," I whispered. I'd made a lot of them myself. Trusting Dave had been one of them.

"Yeah, but yours don't involve..." His voice trailed off as he motioned toward his face.

I knew what he was talking about, and my heart ached for him. I was beginning to understand why he'd walked away. Even though it had hurt me, he'd done it to protect me. He blamed himself for what happened to Blake.

He'd done it because he cared enough about me to keep me from having to make the decision on my own.

But it wasn't fair. I got to decide who was in my life and who was not. He didn't have the right to take that choice away from me. So I decided to act. I was going to take matters into my own hands.

I stepped forward, closing the gap between us. Without hesitating, I wrapped my arms around his neck and rose up on my tiptoes.

"What are you doing?" was all he managed to get out before I pressed my lips to his.

I felt his hesitation, and I wondered if I'd done the wrong thing. Determination built up inside of me as I refused to stop. I wasn't going to allow him to run away again.

I was meant to be with him even if he was too scared to admit the same.

It only took a moment before I felt Jackson relax and slip his hands around my waist. His arms wrapped tightly around me. He squeezed, pulling me up to deepen the kiss. Our lips moved against each other as my fingers found their way into his hair and tangled themselves there.

He was scared. I was scared. We were both broken people. But together, we made something great. We could be something better than either of us could be alone. He had to know that I wasn't going to give up. Not when I found what I'd been looking for.

When he finally pulled back, my world felt hazy. He set my feet down on the ground but kept me tight against his body. I could feel his heartbeat, and it was relaxing.

"Why did you do that?"

I reveled in the sound of his voice, feeling pretty good about myself and the fact that I elicited that reaction from him. I'd been right—he did care about me.

"I didn't want to hear any more excuses about why we can't be together," I said as I drew circles with my finger around his chest. He growled and caught my hand with his. He leaned down and pressed his lips to mine before he slowly kissed along my cheek to my ear.

"You need to stop doing that," he whispered.

The heat from his breath made my entire body shiver.

When he pulled back, I could see both his desire and fear. He studied me before dropping his gaze to the ground.

"What if I hurt Blake again?"

I pressed my finger to his lips. He needed to stop talking like that. "I'll be there. We sort of threw you into the fire. You'll learn his quirks. We'll teach him not to run off. There are solutions." I slid my finger from his lips over to the part of his scar that was visible and gently felt the raised skin.

He closed his eyes as his jaw tightened. My heart ached for this man. I knew what it was like to carry pain, and there was nothing I wanted more than to take that pain away.

"I love you," I whispered before I could stop myself.

Jackson paused before opening his eyes. I could see him staring at me through his sunglasses. "What?" he asked. His voice was so low that I had to lean closer to him to hear what he said.

"I love you."

I thought I would be scared to say that. Uttering those words meant I was giving up the control I needed to feel safe. But the truth was, I felt safe with Jackson. Handing over my heart to him felt right.

I knew he would protect me like I needed him to.

"You love me?"

I nodded, tears filling my eyes. "Yes."

He frowned as he tightened his grip on my waist. Then he dipped down and pressed his lips to mine. I knew that he was worried. I could feel it in his body, see it in his expression. But that didn't matter. I would be here to show him that he was worthy of love until the day I died.

When he pulled back, he rested his forehead on mine. Our breaths matched as we stood there. Then he pulled back and pressed his lips to the tip of my nose.

"I love you, too."

TWENTY-THREE

Penny

$\mathcal{I}$ thought Jackson was going to be my wingman. When I pulled up to Magnolia Inn two days later and got out of the car, I felt confident that I could face Maggie and this town with him by my side. After all, we'd both walked out. We'd both left. We'd both broken off relationships to keep ourselves from getting hurt.

However, after one conversation with Clementine on the way to the inn, Jackson was gone. Apparently, Fiona's court date was today. She was at the courthouse, and Jackson wasn't going to stay behind with that knowledge.

I marveled at the loyalty that man had for her. It was something I'd never experienced in my life. Even though Roger was a good man, when I said the marriage was over, he didn't do much to fight for it.

It wouldn't have mattered if he had. I'd made up my mind and walked out.

With Jackson gone, I was alone. I pulled open the front door and stepped into the foyer of Magnolia Inn, my suitcase trailing behind me.

It was strange. A part of me wanted to walk right back out. To pretend that I was okay with the status quo. It would keep my heart from being broken and keep my daughter from having to decide about allowing me into her life. What if she said no? What if I had misread our relationship, and I was the only one hoping to make it better?

I shook my head. Doubts like that had led me to this situation. If I was going to fight to have a better relationship with my daughter, I needed to start now.

Guests were bustling around the inn. Some were filling plates with Brett's afternoon pastries while others were lingering in the living room, sipping coffee and reading the paper.

I loved how Maggie had created an oasis here. Once you experienced this place, you never wanted to leave.

Hence, my return.

"What are you doing back here?" Archer's deep voice startled me. I turned to see him standing there with an arm full of towels. His brows were furrowed, and his gaze was tight. A stance I'd become all too familiar with when it came to him.

"I'm here to ask for forgiveness." I figured being completely honest was the route to go with him. After all, I was here to start my new life. I was here to make changes that meant something.

Archer stared at me. I could tell that he was sizing me up. So I stood there and let him. He wanted what was best for my daughter, and I couldn't agree more. Maggie deserved the best, and I was determined to be that for her.

It hadn't even fazed me when I walked into Sampson and Scotts the day after Jackson's launch party and put in my formal resignation. They hadn't seemed disappointed —which hurt, but I was learning to get over it. When I left that giant skyscraper of a building with my box of office supplies in hand, I felt…lighter.

I felt free.

Georgette had been thrilled when I called to tell her I was coming to work for her. I loved the sound of her gravelly laugh and her clapping hands. I was ready to get back to my roots and rediscover who Penny really was.

All that was left in New York was my apartment. I had one more month before my lease was up. My goal, now, was to find a place to buy here in Magnolia. Then my adventure could begin.

I just hoped Maggie and Archer wanted to be a part of it.

"Maggie's upstairs making a bed," he said before he sidestepped me and headed around the corner.

Those words were like a giant hug. I was learning more and more about Archer every day, and from what he'd shown me, I liked him. A lot. He was perfect for my daughter. She needed a protector, and Archer was the man for the job.

I left my suitcase behind the reception counter and headed up the stairs. Luckily, it only took a few moments for me to find Maggie. She was in the room in the corner, fluffing pillows. Her hair was pulled back, and her cheeks were pink. Once she wrestled the pillow into its case, she took a moment to blow out her breath and glance around.

That's when she saw me.

"Penny?"

Fear gripped my chest, but I pushed it aside. I was starting new. I was going to be successful here. I was determined to finally allow myself to be happy.

"Hi, Maggie." My gaze slipped down to her wrist, and hope filled my soul when I saw the bracelet I'd made her.

It felt like an open window in the room we'd been stuck in for years.

"I'm sorry." The words tumbled from my lips before I could stop them. Once they were out, I paused, waiting for her reaction.

"You came all this way just to apologize? For what?" Maggie straightened but kept the pillow gripped in her hands.

"Everything. I'm sorry for everything. I'm sorry for not being there. I'm sorry for abandoning you. I'm sorry for not being the mother you deserved." My throat tightened as emotions clung to it. I swallowed before taking in a deep breath. "I want things to change, and I hope you can give me a second chance."

Maggie looked stunned. I waited, hoping that I hadn't scared her off. She had every right to hate me and to tell me off. I wouldn't blame her if she did.

Suddenly, the pillow landed on the bed, and Maggie was making her way across the room. When she got to me, she wrapped her arms around me and pulled me close.

"I forgive you," she whispered as she squeezed me.

I wasn't a particularly touchy-feely person, but for Maggie I'd put that aside. I pulled her into a hug as tears fell down my cheeks.

"I'm a quirky person, and I can't seem to make the right decisions," I said through the tears.

Maggie pulled back to reveal that she was crying as well. She shook her head. "It's okay. I'm not mad."

I reached up to wipe at her tears. She laughed and finished drying her face. "I'm sorry. I'm an emotional wreck."

I shrugged and motioned to my face. "I am as well."

Our giggles subsided as we studied each other. There had been so much emotion in the last minute, that we needed a moment to catch up. Maggie's smile was permanent—as was mine.

She glanced around. "So how long do we have you for?"

Right. I was going to need to address my plans with her. "Well, I was kind of hoping…"

She raised her eyebrows.

Just say it, I chanted in my mind.

"I was hoping that I could stay here until I find a place…" I pointed toward the floor. "Here, in Magnolia."

"You're moving to Magnolia?"

I nodded, waiting for the backlash, waiting for disappointment to fill her gaze.

But it didn't come. Instead she smiled. "I love this plan."

One month later

THERE WAS a soft knock on my door. I brushed down the gold sparkly dress that Maggie and I had picked out on our last trip to New York. We were there to finish packing my apartment and officially move me out of the city I'd lived in most of my life.

We'd had lunch and wandered into numerous over-priced stores. When we saw this dress, we knew it was the one. Despite needing to pay for a house, I decided to buy it—even if the price tag made me want to vomit.

I needed to remember that I wasn't a high-powered editor anymore. My life was going to look drastically different now that I was the owner of a small-town paper.

I couldn't spend my money willy-nilly now.

But Maggie loved this dress, and so did I. So I bought it to make her happy on her wedding day.

"Mom?" Maggie's voice whispered from the other side of the door.

Realizing that my daughter was probably out in the hallway in her wedding dress, I hurried to stand and rushed over to the door. I unlocked it and pulled it open. "What are you doing here?" I asked when I saw my daughter in her fluffy white dress. She looked like a princess.

I was grateful that she'd included me in everything as soon as I got here. She held no grudges. Instead, we picked up right where we'd left off. She wasn't angry or upset, and with my life issues fixed, I was a much more attentive mother.

So much so that she'd gone from calling me Penny to calling me Mom.

She collapsed on the bed and fell backwards. After she exhaled, she said, "I'm panicking just a bit."

I wanted to tell her that she was crushing her curls but decided against it. This was a mom moment, and I was going to live it to the fullest. So I collapsed next to her, lying down so I could look her in the eye. "Why are you panicking?"

She studied me before turning her gaze up toward the ceiling. "What if the reason Sean and I didn't work out was...me?" Her voice drifted off, and I saw the pain that had been left on her heart by that horrible man.

It made me angry. I had half a mind to fly back to New York, track him down, and give him a piece of my mind. But that wasn't going to help my daughter in this moment. The last thing she needed was for me to go mama bear on her ex.

So I reached out and grabbed her hand. After a quick squeeze, I smiled over at her. "Archer is perfect for you. He's better for you than Sean. He loves you, and you love him." My eyes filled with tears, and hers did as well. "Marriage is hard, but with the right person by your side, it makes it worth it."

My heart hurt at those words. Even though I saw them soothe my daughter's worries, something inside of me broke.

Being at my daughter's wedding thrilled me. In a few minutes, I was going to pull her off the bed, and we were going to head out to the beach where the ceremony would take place. I was going to watch as all of her fears melted away when she saw Archer—when he took her hand and wedded her.

I knew she was going to be happy because I was determined to stick around this time. I wanted to be here for the holidays and babies that were sure to come. There was nothing I wanted more in this world than to make up for lost time.

But as I studied my daughter in her wedding dress, getting ready for her second chance, I couldn't help but wonder, was there one in store for me?

Did I deserve a second chance at love?

I sighed as I focused back on the ceiling above me. I should be happy to be where I was. I shouldn't test fate by asking for more.

But no matter how much I tried to convince myself that I didn't need a man—it was a lie.

I wanted a chance at love again.

I just hoped it was in the plans for me.

**

I hope you enjoyed A Magnolia Wedding. I loved writing Fiona's romance and healing the relationship between Maggie and Penny. I have so much in store for Ms. Penny in the next book.

PLUS, Naomi, Jackson's sister will be moving to Magnolia and starting her life over again after a tragic loss in her life.

I can't wait to share their story with you!

Head on over to your favorite platform to grab you copy today HERE!

I ALSO HAVE a complete family saga series that I'm sure you would love! Read the first in the Braxton Brother's Romances, HERE!

Joshua is back in Honey Grove. As a divorced, single dad, he's decided that love is the last thing he needs.

Beth is back in Honey Grove after losing her job and getting dumped.

When Josh's mother, the town's busy body, arranges for Beth to be his nanny, Josh decides to go along with the plan.

Even though Beth is no longer the lanky girl next door, Josh isn't looking for a relationship anyway. He can keep her at a distance. Right?

Everything seems to be working out until their relationship deepens and their arrangement isn't enough anymore.

Too bad her feelings for Josh isn't Beth's only secret.

If you want to connect with Anne-Marie Meyer, join her newsletter and receive Fighting Love with the Cowboy for FREE!

Sign up HERE!

Also join her on these platforms:
Facebook
Instagram
anne-mariemeyer.com